THE ADVENTURES OF MAYA THE BEE

by

WALDEMAR BONSELS

Originally published in 1922.

The Translation of this book was made by ADELE SZOLD SELTZER

The Poems were done into English by ARTHUR GUITERMAN

CHAPTER I

FIRST FLIGHT

The elderly lady-bee who helped the baby-bee Maya when she awoke to life and slipped from her cell was called Cassandra and commanded great respect in the hive. Those were exciting days. A rebellion had broken out in the nation of bees, which the queen was unable to suppress.

While the experienced Cassandra wiped Maya's large bright eyes and tried as best she could to arrange her delicate wings, the big hive hummed and buzzed like a threatening thunderstorm, and the baby-bee found it very warm and said so to her companion.

Cassandra looked about troubled, without replying. It astonished her that the child so soon found something to criticize. But really the child was right: the heat and the pushing and crowding were almost unbearable. Maya saw an endless succession of bees go by in such swarming haste that sometimes one climbed up and over another, or several rolled past together clotted in a ball.

Once the queen-bee approached. Cassandra and Maya were jostled aside. A drone, a friendly young fellow of immaculate appearance, came to their assistance. He nodded to Maya and stroked the shining hairs on his breast rather nervously with his foreleg. (The bees use their forelegs as arms and hands.)

"The crash will come," he said to Cassandra. "The revolutionists will leave the city. A new queen has already been proclaimed."

Cassandra scarcely noticed him. She did not even thank him for his help, and Maya felt keenly conscious that the old lady was not a bit nice to the young gentleman. The child was a little afraid to ask questions, the impressions were coming so thick and fast; they threatened to overwhelm her. The general excitement got into her blood, and she set up a fine, distinct buzzing.

"What do you mean by that?" said Cassandra. "Isn't there noise enough as it is?"

Maya subsided at once, and looked at Cassandra questioningly.

"Come here, child, we'll see if we cannot quiet down a bit." Cassandra took Maya by her gleaming wings, which were still soft and new and marvelously transparent, and shoved her into an almost deserted corner beside a few honeycombs filled with honey.

Maya stood still and held on to one of the cells.

"It smells delicious here," she observed.

Her remark seemed to fluster the old lady again.

"You must learn to wait, child," she replied. "I have brought up several hundred young bees this spring and given them lessons for their first flight, but I haven't come across another one that was as pert and forward as you are. You seem to be an exceptional nature."

Maya blushed and stuck the two dainty fingers of her hand in her mouth.

"Exceptional nature--what is an exceptional nature?" she asked shyly.

"Oh, *that's* not nice," cried Cassandra, referring not to Maya's question, which she had scarcely heeded, but to the child's sticking her fingers in her mouth. "Now, listen. Listen very carefully to what I am going to tell you. I can devote only a short time to you. Other baby-bees have already slipped out, and the only helper I have on this floor is Turka, and Turka is dreadfully overworked and for the last few days has been complaining of a buzzing in her ears. Sit down here."

Maya obeyed, with great brown eyes fastened on her teacher.

"The first rule that a young bee must learn," said Cassandra, and sighed, "is that every bee, in whatever it thinks and does, must be like the other bees and must always have the good of all in mind. In our order of society, which we have held to be the right one from time immemorial and which couldn't have been better preserved than it has been, this rule is the one fundamental basis for the well-being of the state. To-morrow you will fly out of the hive, an older bee will accompany you. At first you will be allowed to fly only short stretches and you will have to observe everything, very carefully, so that you can find your way back home again. Your companion will show you the hundred flowers and blossoms that yield the best nectar. You'll have to learn them by heart. This is something no bee can escape doing.-- Here, you may as well learn the first line right away--clover and honeysuckle. Repeat it. Say 'clover and honeysuckle.'"

"I can't," said little Maya. "It's awfully hard. I'll see the flowers later anyway."

Cassandra opened her old eyes wide and shook her head.

"You'll come to a bad end," she sighed. "I can foresee that already."

"Am I supposed later on to gather nectar all day long?" asked Maya.

Cassandra fetched a deep sigh and gazed at the baby-bee seriously and sadly. She seemed to be thinking of her own toilsome life--toil from beginning to end, nothing but toil. Then she spoke in a changed voice, with a loving look in her eyes for the child.

"My dear little Maya, there will be other things in your life--the sunshine, lofty green trees, flowery heaths, lakes of silver, rushing, glistening waterways, the heavens blue and radiant, and perhaps even human beings, the highest and most perfect of Nature's creations. Because of all these glories your work will become a joy. Just think--all that lies ahead of you, dear heart. You have good reason to be happy."

"I'm so glad," said Maya, "that's what I want to be."

Cassandra smiled kindly. In that instant--why, she did not know--she conceived a peculiar affection for the little bee, such as she could not recall ever having felt for any child-bee before. And that, probably, is how it came about that she told Maya more than a bee usually hears on the first day of its life. She gave her various special bits of advice, warned her against the dangers of the wicked world, and named the bees' most dangerous enemies. At the end she spoke long of human beings, and implanted the first love for them in the child's heart and the germ of a great longing to know them.

"Be polite and agreeable to every insect you meet," she said in conclusion, "then you will learn more from them than I have told you to-day. But beware of the wasps and hornets. The hornets are our most formidable enemy, and the wickedest, and the wasps are a useless tribe of thieves, without home or religion. We are a stronger, more powerful nation, while they steal and murder wherever they can. You may use your sting upon insects, to defend yourself and inspire respect, but if you insert it in a warm-blooded animal, especially a human being, you will die, because it will remain sticking in the skin and will break off. So do not sting warm-blooded creatures except in dire need, and then do it without flinching or fear of death. For it is to our courage as well as our wisdom that we bees owe the universal respect and esteem in which we are held. And now good-by, Maya dear. Good luck to you. Be faithful to your people and your queen."

The little bee nodded yes, and returned her old monitor's kiss and embrace. She went to bed in a flutter of secret joy and excitement and could scarcely fall asleep from curiosity. For the next day she was to know the great, wide world, the sun, the sky and the flowers.

Meanwhile the bee-city had quieted down. A large part of the younger bees had now left the kingdom to found a new city; but for a long time the droning of the great swarm could be heard outside in the sunlight. It was not from arrogance or evil intent against the queen that these had quitted; it was because the population had grown to such a size that there was no longer room for all the inhabitants, and it was impossible to store a sufficient food-supply of honey to feed them all over the winter. You see, according to a government treaty of long standing, a large part of the honey gathered in summer had to be delivered up to human beings, who in return assured the welfare of the bee-state, provided for the peace and safety of the bees, and gave them shelter against the cold in winter.

"The sun has risen!"

The joyous call sounding in Maya's ears awoke her out of sleep the next morning. She jumped up and joined a lady working-bee.

"Delighted," said the lady cordially. "You may fly with me."

At the gate, where there was a great pushing and crowding, they were held up by the sentinels, one of whom gave Maya the password without which no bee was admitted into the city.

"Be sure to remember it," he said, "and good luck to you."

Outside the city gates, a flood of sunlight assailed the little bee, a brilliance of green and gold, so rich and warm and resplendent that she had to close her eyes, not knowing what to say or do from sheer delight.

"Magnificent! It really is," she said to her companion. "Do we fly into that?"

"Right ahead!" answered the lady-bee.

Maya raised her little head and moved her pretty new wings. Suddenly she felt the flying-board on which she had been sitting sink down, while the ground seemed to be gliding away behind, and the large green domes of the tree-tops seemed to be coming toward her.

Her eyes sparkled, her heart rejoiced.

"I am flying," she cried. "It cannot be anything else. What I am doing must be flying. Why, it's splendid, perfectly splendid!"

"Yes, you're flying," said the lady-bee, who had difficulty in keeping up with the child. "Those are linden-trees, those toward which we are flying, the lindens in our castle park. You can always tell where our city is by those lindens. But you're flying so fast, Maya."

"Fast?" said Maya. "How can one fly fast enough? Oh, how sweet the sunshine smells!"

"No," replied her companion, who was rather out of breath, "it's not the sunshine, it's the flowers that smell.-- But please, don't go so fast, else I'll drop behind. Besides, at this pace you won't observe things and be able to find your way back."

But little Maya transported by the sunshine and the joy of living, did not hear. She felt as though she were darting like an arrow through a green-shimmering sea of light, to greater and greater splendor. The bright flowers seemed to call to her, the still, sunlit distances lured her on, and the blue sky blessed her joyous young flight.

"Never again will it be as beautiful as it is to-day," she thought. "I *can't* turn back. I can't think of anything except the sun."

Beneath her the gay pictures kept changing, the peaceful landscape slid by slowly, in broad stretches.

"The sun must be all of gold," thought the baby-bee.

Coming to a large garden, which seemed to rest in

blossoming clouds of cherry-tree, hawthorn, and lilacs, she let herself down to earth, dead-tired, and dropped in a bed of red tulips, where she held on to one of the big flowers. With a great sigh of bliss she pressed herself against the blossom-wall and looked up to the deep blue of the sky through the gleaming edges of the flowers.

"Oh, how beautiful it is out here in the great world, a thousand times more beautiful than in the dark hive. I'll never go back there again to carry honey or make wax. No, indeed, I'll never do that. I want to see and know the world in bloom. I am not like the other bees, my heart is meant for pleasure and surprises, experiences and adventures. I will not be afraid of any dangers. Haven't I got strength and courage and a sting?"

She laughed, bubbling over with delight, and took a deep draught of nectar out of the flower of the tulip.

"Grand," she thought. "It's glorious to be alive."

Ah, if little Maya had had an inkling of the many dangers and hardships that lay ahead of her, she would certainly have thought twice. But never dreaming of such things, she stuck to her resolve.

Soon tiredness overcame her, and she fell asleep. When she awoke, the sun was gone, twilight lay upon the land. A bit of alarm, after all. Maya's heart went a little faster. Hesitatingly she crept out of the flower, which was about to close up for the night, and hid herself away under a leaf high up in the top of an old tree, where she went to sleep, thinking in the utmost confidence:

"I'm not afraid. I won't be afraid right at the very start. The sun is coming round again; that's certain; Cassandra said so. The thing to do is to go to sleep quietly and sleep well."

CHAPTER II

THE HOUSE OF THE ROSE

By the time Maya awoke, it was full daylight. She felt a little chilly under her big green leaf, and stiff in her limbs, so that her first movements were slow and clumsy. Clinging to a vein of the leaf she let her wings quiver and vibrate, to limber them up and shake off the dust; then she smoothed her fair hair, wiped her large eyes clean, and crept, warily, down to the edge of the leaf, where she paused and looked around.

The glory and the glow of the morning sun were dazzling. Though Maya's resting-place still lay in cool shadow, the leaves overhead shone like green gold.

"Oh, you glorious world," thought the little bee.

Slowly, one by one, the experiences of the previous day came back to her--all the beauties she had seen and all the risks she had run. She remained firm in her resolve not to return to the hive. To be sure,

when she thought of Cassandra, her heart beat fast,
though it was not very likely that Cassandra would
ever find her.-- No, no, to her there was no joy in
forever having to fly in and out of the hive, carrying
honey and making wax. This was clear, once and
for all. She wanted to be happy and free and enjoy
life in her own way. Come what might, she would
take the consequences.

Thus lightly thought Maya, the truth being that she
had no real idea of the things that lay in store for
her.

Afar off in the sunshine something glimmered red.
A lurking impatience seized the little bee.
Moreover, she felt hungry. So, courageously, with a
loud joyous buzz, she swung out of her hiding-place
into the clear, glistening air and the warm sunlight,
and made straight for the red patch that seemed to
nod and beckon. When she drew near she smelled a
perfume so sweet that it almost robbed her of her
senses, and she was hardly able to reach the large
red flower. She let herself down on the outermost of
its curved petals and clung to it tightly. At the
gentle tipping of the petal a shining silver sphere
almost as big as herself, came rolling toward her,
transparent and gleaming in all the colors of the
rainbow. Maya was dreadfully frightened, yet
fascinated too by the splendor of the cool silver
sphere, which rolled by her, balanced on the edge of
the petal, leapt into the sunshine, and fell down in
the grass. Oh, oh! The beautiful ball had shivered
into a score of wee pearls. Maya uttered a little cry
of terror. But the tiny round fragments made such a
bright, lively glitter in the grass, and ran down the

blades in such twinkling, sparkling little drops like diamonds in the lamplight, that she was reassured.

She turned towards the inside of the calix. A beetle, a little smaller than herself, with brown wing-sheaths and a black breastplate, was sitting at the entrance. He kept his place unperturbed, and looked at her seriously, though by no means unamiably. Maya bowed politely.

"Did the ball belong to you?" she asked, and receiving no reply added: "I am very sorry I threw it down."

"Do you mean the dewdrop?" smiled the beetle, rather superior. "You needn't worry about that. I had taken a drink already and my wife never drinks water, she has kidney trouble.-- What are you doing here?"

"What is this wonderful flower?" asked Maya, not answering the beetle's question. "Would you be good enough to tell me its name?"

Remembering Cassandra's advice she was as polite as possible.

The beetle moved his shiny head in his dorsal plate, a thing he could do easily without the least discomfort, as his head fitted in perfectly and glided back and forth without a click.

"You seem to be only of yesterday?" he said, and laughed--not so very politely. Altogether there was something about him that struck Maya as unrefined.

The bees had more culture and better manners. Yet he seemed to be a good-natured fellow, because, seeing Maya's blush of embarrassment, he softened to her childish ignorance.

"It's a rose," he explained indulgently. "So now you know.-- We moved in four days ago, and since we moved in, it has flourished wonderfully under our care.-- Won't you come in?"

Maya hesitated, then conquered her misgivings and took a few steps forward. He pressed aside a bright petal, Maya entered, and she and the beetle walked beside each other through the narrow chambers with their subdued light and fragrant walls.

"What a charming home!" exclaimed Maya, genuinely taken with the place. "The perfume is positively intoxicating."

Maya's admiration pleased the beetle.

"It takes wisdom to know where to live," he said, and smiled good-naturedly. "'Tell me where you live and I'll tell you what you're worth,' says an old adage.-- Would you like some nectar?"

"Oh," Maya burst out, "I'd love some."

The beetle nodded and disappeared behind one of the walls. Maya looked about. She was happy. She pressed her cheeks and little hands against the dainty red hangings and took deep breaths of the delicious perfume, in an ecstasy of delight at being permitted to stop in such a beautiful dwelling.

"It certainly is a great joy to be alive," she thought.
"And there's no comparison between the dingy,
crowded stories in which the bees live and work
and this house. The very quiet here is splendid."

Suddenly there was a loud sound of scolding behind
the walls. It was the beetle growling excitedly in
great anger. He seemed to be hustling and pushing
someone along roughly, and Maya caught the
following, in a clear, piping voice full of fright and
mortification.

"Of course, because I'm alone, you dare to lay hands
on me. But wait and see what you get when I bring
my associates along. You are a ruffian. Very well, I
am going. But remember, I called you a ruffian.
You'll never forget *that*."

The stranger's emphatic tone, so sharp and vicious,
frightened Maya dreadfully. In a few moments she
heard the sound of someone running out.

The beetle returned and sullenly flung down some
nectar.

"An outrage," he said. "You can't escape those
vermin anywhere. They don't allow you a moment's
peace."

Maya was so hungry she forgot to thank him and
took a mouthful of nectar and chewed, while the
beetle wiped the perspiration from his forehead and
slightly loosened his upper armor so as to catch his
breath.

"Who was that?" mumbled Maya, with her mouth still full.

"Please empty your mouth--finish chewing and swallowing your nectar. One can't understand a word you say."

Maya obeyed, but the excited owner of the house gave her no time to repeat her question.

"It was an ant," he burst out angrily. "Do those ants think we save and store up hour after hour only for them! The idea of going right into the pantry without a how-do-you-do or a by-your-leave! It makes me furious. If I didn't realize that the ill-mannered creatures actually didn't know better, I wouldn't hesitate a second to call them--thieves!"

At this he suddenly remembered his own manners.

"I beg your pardon," he said, turning to Maya, "I forgot to introduce myself. My name is Peter, of the family of rose-beetles."

"My name is Maya," said the little bee shyly. "I am delighted to make your acquaintance." She looked at Peter closely; he was bowing repeatedly, and spreading his feelers like two little brown fans. That pleased Maya immensely.

"You have the most fascinating feelers," she said, "simply sweet...."

"Well, yes," observed Peter, flattered, "people do

think a lot of them. Would you like to see the other side?"

"If I may."

The rose-beetle turned his fan-shaped feelers to one side and let a ray of sunlight glide over them.

"Great, don't you think?" he asked.

"I shouldn't have thought anything like them possible," rejoined Maya. "My own feelers are very plain."

"Well, yes," observed Peter, "to each his own. By way of compensation you certainly have beautiful eyes, and the color of your body, the gold of your body, is not to be sneezed at."

Maya beamed. Peter was the first person to tell her she had any good looks. Life was great. She was happy as a lark, and helped herself to some more nectar.

"An excellent quality of honey," she remarked.

"Take some more," said Peter, rather amazed by his little guest's appetite. "Rose-juice of the first vintage. One has to be careful and not spoil one's stomach. There's some dew left, too, if you're thirsty."

"Thank you so much," said Maya. "I'd like to fly now, if you will permit me."

The rose-beetle laughed.

"Flying, always flying," he said. "It's in the blood of you bees. I don't understand such a restless way of living. There's some advantage in staying in one place, too, don't you think?"

Peter courteously held the red curtain aside.

"I'll go as far as our observation petal with you," he said. "It makes an excellent place to fly from."

"Oh, thank you," said Maya, "I can fly from anywhere."

"That's where you have the advantage over me," replied Peter. "I have some difficulty in unfolding my lower wings." He shook her hand and held the last curtain aside for her.

"Oh, the blue sky!" rejoiced Maya. "Good-by."

"So long," called Peter, remaining on the top petal to see Maya rise rapidly straight up to the sky in the golden sunlight and the clear, pure air of the morning. With a sigh he returned, pensive, to his cool rose-dwelling, for though it was still early he was feeling rather warm. He sang his morning song to himself, and it hummed in the red sheen of the petals and the radiance of the spring day that slowly mounted and spread over the blossoming earth.

Gold and green are field and tree, Warm in summer's glow; All is bright and fair to see While the roses blow.

What or why the world may be Who can guess or know? All my world is glad and free While the roses blow.

Brief, they say, my time of glee; With the roses I go; Yes, but life is good to me While the roses blow.

CHAPTER III

THE LAKE

"Dear me," thought Maya, after she had flown off, "oh, dear me, I forgot to ask Mr. Peter about human beings. A gentleman of his wide experience could certainly have told me about them. But perhaps I'll meet one myself to-day." Full of high spirits and in a happy mood of adventure, she let her bright eyes rove over the wide landscape that lay spread out below in all its summer splendor.

She came to a large garden gleaming with a thousand colors. On her way she met many insects, who sang out greetings, and wished her a pleasant journey and a good harvest.-- But every time she met a bee, her heart went pit-a-pat. After all she felt a little guilty to be idle, and was afraid of coming upon acquaintances. Soon, however, she saw that the bees paid not the slightest attention to her.

Then all of a sudden the world seemed to turn
upside down. The heavens shone *below* her, in
endless depths. At first she was dreadfully
frightened; she thought she had flown too far up and
lost her way in the sky. But presently she noticed
that the trees were mirrored on the edge of the
terrestrial sky, and to her entrancement she realized
that she was looking at a great serene basin of water
which lay blue and clear in the peaceful morning.
She let herself down close to the surface. There was
her image flying in reflection, the lovely gold of her
body shining at her from the water, her bright wings
glittering like clear glass. And she observed that she
held her little legs properly against her body, as
Cassandra had taught her to do.

"It's bliss to be flying over the surface of water like
this. It is, really," she thought.

Big fish and little fish swam about in the clear
element, or seemed to float idly. Maya took good
care not to go too close; she knew there was danger
to bees from the race of fishes.

On the opposite shore she was attracted by the
water-lilies and the rushes, the water-lilies with
their large round leaves lying outspread on the
water like green plates, and the rushes with their
sun-warmed, reedy stalks.

She picked out a leaf well-concealed under the tall
blades of the rushes. It lay in almost total shade,
except for two round spots like gold coins; the
rushes swayed above in the full sunlight.

"Glorious," said the little bee, "perfectly glorious."

She began to tidy herself. Putting both arms up behind her head she pulled it forward as if to tear it off, but was careful not to pull too hard, just enough to scrape away the dust; then, with her little hind legs, she stroked and dragged down her wing-sheaths, which sprang back in position looking beautifully bright and glossy.

Just as she had completed her toilet a small steely blue-bottle came and alighted on the leaf beside her. He looked at her in surprise.

"What are you doing here on my leaf?" he demanded.

Maya was startled.

"Is there any objection to a person's just resting here a moment or two?"

Maya remembered Cassandra's telling her that the nation of bees commanded great respect in the insect world. Now she was going to see if it was true; she was going to see if she, Maya, could compel respect. Nevertheless her heart beat a little faster because her tone had been very loud and peremptory.

But actually the blue-bottle was frightened. He showed it plainly. When he saw that Maya wasn't going to let anyone lay down the law to her he backed down. With a surly buzz he swung himself on to a blade that curved above Maya's leaf, and said in a much politer tone, talking down to her out of the sunshine:

"You ought to be working. As a bee you certainly ought. But if you want to rest, all right. I'll wait here."

"There are plenty of leaves," observed Maya.

"All rented," said the blue-bottle. "Now-a-days one is happy to be able to call a piece of ground one's own. If my predecessor hadn't been snapped up by a frog two days ago, I should still be without a proper place to live in. It's not very pleasant to have to hunt up a different lodging every night. Not everyone has such a well-ordered state as you bees. But permit me to introduce myself. My name is Jack Christopher."

Maya was silent with terror, thinking how awful it must be to fall into the clutches of a frog.

"Are there many frogs in the lake?" she asked and drew to the very middle of the leaf so as not to be seen from the water.

The blue-bottle laughed.

"You are giving yourself unnecessary trouble," he jeered. "The frog can see you from below when the sun shines, because then the leaf is transparent. He sees you sitting on my leaf, perfectly."

Beset by the awful idea that maybe a big frog was

squatting right under her leaf staring at her with his bulging hungry eyes, Maya was about to fly off when something dreadful happened, something for which she was totally unprepared. In the confusion of the first moment she could not make out just exactly what *was* happening. She only heard a loud rustling like the wind in dry leaves, then a singing whistle, a loud angry hunter's cry. And a fine, transparent shadow glided over her leaf. Now she saw--saw fully, and her heart stood still in terror. A great, glittering dragon-fly had caught hold of poor Jack Christopher and held him tight in its large, fangs, sharp as a knife. The blade of the rush bent low beneath their weight. Maya could see them hovering above her and also mirrored in the clear water below. Jack's screams tore her heart. Without thinking, she cried:

"Let the blue-bottle go, at once, whoever you are. You have no right to interfere with people's habits. You have no right to be so arbitrary."

The dragon-fly released Jack from its fangs, but still held him fast with its arms, and turned its head toward Maya. She was fearfully frightened by its large, grave eyes and vicious pincers, but the glittering of its body and wings fascinated her. They flashed like glass and water and precious stones. The horrifying thing was its huge size. How could she have been so bold? She was all a-tremble.

"Why, what's the matter, child?" The dragon-fly's tone, surprisingly, was quite friendly.

"Let him go," cried Maya, and tears came into her

eyes. "His name is Jack Christopher."

The dragon-fly smiled.

"Why, little one?" it said, putting on an interested air, though most condescending.

Maya stammered helplessly:

"Oh, he's such a nice, elegant gentleman, and he's never done you any harm so far as I know."

The dragon-fly regarded Jack Christopher contemplatively.

"Yes, he *is* a dear little fellow," it replied tenderly and--bit Jack's head off.

Maya thought she was losing her senses. For a long time she couldn't utter a sound. In horror she listened to the munching and crunching above her as the body of Jack Christopher the blue-bottle was being dismembered.

"Don't put on so," said the dragon-fly with its mouth full, chewing. "Your sensitiveness doesn't impress me. Are you bees any better? What do you do? Evidently you are very young still and haven't looked about in your own house. When the massacre of the drones takes place in the summer, the rest of the world is no less shocked and horrified, and *I* think with greater justification."

Maya asked:

"Have you finished up there?" She did not dare to raise her eyes.

"One leg still left," replied the dragon-fly.

"Do please swallow it. Then I'll answer you," cried Maya, who knew that the drones in the hive *had* to be killed off in the summer, and was provoked by the dragon-fly's stupidity. "But don't you dare to come a step closer. If you do I'll use my sting on you."

Little Maya had really lost her temper. It was the first time she had mentioned her sting and the first time she felt glad that she possessed the weapon.

The dragon-fly threw her a wicked glance. It had finished its meal and sat with its head slightly ducked, fixing Maya with its eyes and looking like a beast of prey about to pounce. The little bee was quite calm now. Where she got her courage from she couldn't have told, but she was no longer afraid. She set up a very fine clear buzzing as she had once heard a sentinel do when a wasp came near the entrance of the hive.

The dragon-fly said slowly and threateningly:

"Dragon-flies live on the best terms with the nation of bees."

"Very sensible in them," flashed Maya.

"Do you mean to insinuate that I am afraid of you--I

of you?" With a jerk the dragon-fly let go of the rush, which sprang back into its former position, and flew off with a whirr and sparkle of its wings, straight down to the surface of the water, where it made a superb appearance reflected in the mirror of the lake. You'd have thought there were two dragon-flies. Both moved their crystal wings so swiftly and finely that it seemed as though a brilliant sheen of silver were streaming around them.

Maya quite forgot her grief over poor Jack Christopher and all sense of her own danger.

"How lovely! How lovely!" she cried enthusiastically, clapping her hands.

"Do you mean me?" The dragon-fly spoke in astonishment, but quickly added: "Yes, I must admit I am fairly presentable. Yesterday I was flying along the brook, and you should have heard some human beings who were lying on the bank rave over me."

"Human beings!" exclaimed Maya. "Oh my, did you see human beings?"

"Of course," answered the dragon-fly. "But you'll be very interested to know my name, I'm sure. My name is Loveydear, of the order Odonata, of the family Libellulidæ."

"Oh, do tell me about human beings," implored Maya, after she had introduced herself.

The dragon-fly seemed won over. She seated herself on the leaf beside Maya. And the little bee let her, knowing Miss Loveydear would be careful not to come too close.

"Have human beings a sting?" she asked.

"Good gracious, what would they do with a sting! No, they have worse weapons against us, and they are very dangerous. There isn't a soul who isn't afraid of them, especially of the little ones whose two legs show--the boys."

"Do they try to catch you?" asked Maya, breathless with excitement.

"Yes, can't you understand why?" Miss Loveydear glanced at her wings. "I have seldom met a human being who hasn't tried to catch me."

"But why?" asked Maya in a tremor.

"You see," said Miss Loveydear, with a modest smirk and a drooping, sidewise glance, "there's something attractive about us dragon-flies. That's the only reason I know. Some members of our family who let themselves be caught went through the cruellest tortures and finally died."

"Were they eaten up?"

"No, no, not exactly that," said Miss Loveydear comfortingly. "So far as is known, man does not feed on dragon-flies. But sometimes he has murderous desires, a lust for killing, which will probably never be explained. You may not believe it, but cases have actually occurred of the so-called boy-men catching dragon-flies and pulling off their legs and wings for pure pleasure. You doubt it, don't you?"

"Of course I doubt it," cried Maya indignantly.

Miss Loveydear shrugged her glistening shoulders. Her face looked old with knowledge.

"Oh," she said after a pause, grieving and pale, "if only one could speak of these things openly. I had a brother who gave promise of a splendid future, only, I'm sorry to say, he was a little reckless and dreadfully curious. A boy once threw a net over him, a net fastened to a long pole.-- Who would dream of a thing like that? Tell me. Would you?"

"No," said the little bee, "never. I should never have thought of such a thing."

The dragon-fly looked at her.

"A black cord was tied round his waist between his wings, so that he could fly, but not fly away, not escape. Each time my brother thought he had got his liberty, he would be jerked back horribly within the boy's reach."

Maya shook her head.

"You don't dare even think of it," she whispered.

"If a day passes when I don't think of it," said the dragon-fly, "I am sure to dream of it. One misfortune followed another. My brother soon died." Miss Loveydear heaved a deep sigh.

"What did he die of?" asked Maya, in genuine sympathy.

Miss Loveydear could not reply at once. Great tears welled up and rolled down her cheeks.

"He was stuck in a pocket," she sobbed. "No one can stand being stuck in a pocket."

"But what is a pocket?" Maya could hardly take in so many new and awful things all at once.

"A pocket," Miss Loveydear explained, "is a store-room that men have in their outer hide.-- And what else do you think was in the pocket when my brother was stuck into it? Oh, the dreadful company in which my poor brother had to draw his last breath! You'll never guess!"

"No," said Maya, all in a quiver, "no, I don't think I can.-- Honey, perhaps?"

"Not likely," observed Miss Loveydear with an air of mingled importance and distress. "You'll seldom find honey in the pockets of human beings. I'll tell you.-- A frog was in the pocket, and a pen-knife, and a carrot. Well?"

"Horrible," whispered Maya.-- "What *is* a pen-knife?"

"A pen-knife, in a way, is a human being's sting, an artificial one. They are denied a sting by nature, so they try to imitate it.-- The frog, thank goodness, was nearing his end. One eye was gone, one leg was broken, and his lower jaw was dislocated. Yet, for all that, the moment my brother was stuck in the pocket he hissed at him out of his crooked mouth:

"'As soon as I am well, I will swallow you.'

"With his remaining eye he glared at my brother, and in the half-light of the prison you can imagine what an effect the look he gave him must have had-- fearful!-- Then something even more horrible happened. The pocket was suddenly shaken, my brother was pressed against the dying frog and his wings stuck to its cold, wet body. He went off in a faint.-- Oh, the misery of it! There are no words to describe it."

"How did you find all this out?" Maya was so horrified she could scarcely frame the question.

"I'll tell you," replied Miss Loveydear. "After a while the boy got hungry and dug into his pocket for the carrot. It was under my brother and the frog, and the boy threw them away first.-- I heard my brother's cry for help, and found him lying beside the frog on the grass. I reached him only in time to hear the whole story before he breathed his last. He put his arms round my neck and kissed me farewell. Then he died--bravely and without complaining, like a little hero. When his crushed wings had given their last quiver, I laid an oak leaf over his body and went to look for a sprig of forget-me-nots to put upon his grave. 'Sleep well, my little brother,' I cried, and flew off in the quiet of the evening. I flew toward the two red suns, the one in the sky and the one in the lake. No one has ever felt as sad and solemn as I did then.-- Have you ever had a sorrow in your life? Perhaps you'll tell me about it some other time."

"No," said Maya. "As a matter of fact, until now I have always been happy."

"You may thank your lucky stars," said Miss Loveydear with a note of disappointment in her voice.

Maya asked about the frog.

"Oh, *him*," said Miss Loveydear. "He, it is presumed, met with the end he deserved. The hard-heartedness of him, to frighten a dying person! When I found him on the grass beside my brother, he was trying to get away. But on account of his broken leg and one eye gone, all he could do was hop round in a circle and hop round in a circle. He looked too comical for words. 'The stork'll soon get ye,' I called to him as I flew away."

"Poor frog!" said little Maya.

"Poor frog! Poor frog indeed! That's going too far. Pitying a frog. The idea! To feel sorry for a frog is like clipping your own wings. You seem to have no principles."

"Perhaps. But it's hard for me to see *any* one suffer."

"Oh"--Miss Loveydear comforted her--"that's because you're so young. You'll learn to bear it in time. Cheerio, my dear.-- But I must be getting into the sunshine. It's pretty cold here. Good-by!"

A faint rustle and the gleam of a thousand colors, lovely pale colors like the glints in running water and clear gems.

Miss Loveydear swung through the green rushes out over the surface of the water. Maya heard her singing in the sunshine. She stood and listened. It was a fine song, with something of the melancholy sweetness of a folksong, and it filled the little bee's heart with mingled happiness and sadness.

Softly flows the lovely stream Touched by morning's rosy gleam Through the alders darted, Where the rushes bend and sway, Where the water-lilies say "We are golden-hearted!"

Warm the scent the west-wind brings, Bright the sun upon my wings, Joy among the flowers! Though my life may not be long, Golden summer, take my song! Thanks for perfect hours!

"Listen!" a white butterfly called to its friend. "Listen to the song of the dragon-fly." The light creatures rocked close to Maya, and rocked away again into the radiant blue day. Then Maya also lifted her wings, buzzed farewell to the silvery lake, and flew inland.

CHAPTER IV

EFFIE AND BOBBIE

When Maya awoke the next morning in the corolla of a blue canterbury bell, she heard a fine, faint rustling in the air and felt her blossom-bed quiver as from a tiny, furtive tap-tapping. Through the open corolla came a damp whiff of grass and earth, and the air was quite chill. In some apprehension, she took a little pollen from the yellow stamens, scrupulously performed her toilet, then, warily, picking her steps, ventured to the outer edge of the drooping blossom. It was raining! A fine cool rain was coming down with a light plash, covering everything all round with millions of bright silver pearls, which clung to the leaves and flowers, rolled down the green paths of the blades of grass, and refreshed the brown soil.

What a change in the world! It was the first time in the child-bee's young life that she had seen rain. It filled her with wonder; it delighted her. Yet she was a little troubled. She remembered Cassandra's warning never to fly abroad in the rain. It must be difficult, she realized, to move your wings when the drops beat them down. And the cold really hurt, and she missed the quiet golden sunshine that gladdened the earth and made it a place free from all care.

It seemed to be very early still. The animal life in the grass was just beginning. From the concealment of her lofty bluebell Maya commanded a splendid view of the social life coming awake beneath. Watching it she forgot, for the moment, her anxiety and mounting homesickness. It was too amusing for anything to be safe in a hiding-place, high up, and look down on the doings of the grass-dwellers below.

Slowly, however, her thoughts went back--back to the home she had left, to the bee-state, and to the protection of its close solidarity. There, on this rainy day, the bees would be sitting together, glad of the day of rest, doing a little construction here and there on the cells, or feeding the larvæ. Yet, on the whole, the hive was very quiet and Sunday-like when it rained. Only, sometimes messengers would fly out to see how the weather was and from what quarter the wind was blowing. The queen would go about her kingdom from story to story, testing things, bestowing a word of praise or blame, laying an egg here and there, and bringing happiness with her royal presence wherever she went. She might pat one of the younger bees on the head to show her approval of what it had already done, or she might ask it about its new experiences. How delighted a bee would be to catch a glance or receive a gracious word from the queen!

Oh, thought Maya, how happy it made you to be able to count yourself one in a community like that, to feel that everybody respected you, and you had the powerful protection of the state. Here, out in the world, lonely and exposed, she ran great risks of her life. She was cold, too. And supposing the rain were to keep up! What would she do, how could she find something to eat? There was scarcely any honey-juice in the canterbury bell, and the pollen would soon give out.

For the first time Maya realized how necessary the sunshine is for a life of vagabondage. Hardly anyone would set out on adventure, she thought, if it weren't for the sunshine. The very recollection of it was cheering, and she glowed with secret pride that she had had the daring to start life on her own hook. The number of things she had already seen and experienced! More, ever so much more, than the other bees were likely to know in a whole lifetime. Experience was the most precious thing in life, worth any sacrifice, she thought.

A troop of migrating ants were passing by, and singing as they marched through the cool forest of grass. They seemed to be in a hurry. Their crisp morning song, in rhythm with their march, touched the little bee's heart with melancholy.

Few our days on earth shall be, Fast the moments flit; First-class robbers such as we Do not care a bit!

They were extraordinarily well armed and looked saucy, bold and dangerous.

The song died away under the leaves of the coltsfoot. But some mischief seemed to have been done there. A rough, hoarse voice sounded, and the small leaves of a young dandelion were energetically thrust aside. Maya saw a corpulent blue beetle push its way out. It looked like a half-sphere of dark metal, shimmering with lights of blue and green and occasional black. It may have been two or even three times her size. Its hard sheath looked as though nothing could destroy it, and its deep voice positively frightened you.

The song of the soldiers, apparently, had roused him out of sleep. He was cross. His hair was still rumpled, and he rubbed the sleep out of his cunning little blue eyes.

"Make way, *I'm* coming. Make way."

He seemed to think that people should step aside at the mere announcement of his approach.

"Thank the Lord I'm not in his way," thought Maya, feeling very safe in her high, swaying nook of concealment. Nevertheless her heart went pit-a-pat, and she withdrew a little deeper into the flower-bell.

The beetle moved with a clumsy lurch through the wet grass, presenting a not exactly elegant appearance. Directly under Maya's blossom was a withered leaf. Here he stopped, shoved the leaf aside, and made a step backward. Maya saw a hole in the ground.

"Well," she thought, all a-gog with curiosity, "the things there *are* in the world. I never thought of such a thing. Life's not long enough for all there is to see."

She kept very quiet. The only sound was the soft pelting of the rain. Then she heard the beetle calling down the hole:

"If you want to go hunting with me, you'll have to make up your mind to get right up. It's already bright daylight." He was feeling so very superior for having waked up first that it was hard for him to be pleasant.

A few moments passed before the answer came. Then Maya heard a thin, chirping voice rise out of the hole.

"For goodness' sake, do close the door up there. It's raining in."

The beetle obeyed. He stood in an expectant attitude, his head cocked a little to one side, and squinted through the crack.

"Please hurry," he grumbled.

Maya was tense with eagerness to see what sort of a creature would come out of the hole. She crept so far out on the edge of the blossom that a drop of rain fell on her shoulder, and gave her a start. She wiped herself dry.

Below her the withered leaf heaved; a brown insect crept out, slowly. Maya thought it was the queerest specimen she had ever seen. It had a plump body, set on extremely thin, slow-moving legs, and a fearfully thick head, with little upright feelers. It looked flustered.

"Good morning, Effie dear." The beetle went slim with politeness. He was all politeness, and his body seemed really slim. "How did you sleep? How did you sleep, my precious--my all?"

Effie took his hand rather stonily.

"It can't be, Bobbie," she said. "I can't go with you. We're creating too much talk."

Poor Bobbie looked quite alarmed.

"I don't understand," he stammered. "I don't understand.-- Is our new-found happiness to be wrecked by such nonsense? Effie, think--think the thing over. What do *you* care *what* people say? You have your hole, you can creep into it whenever you like, and if you go down far enough, you won't hear a syllable."

Effie smiled a sad, superior smile.

"Bobbie, you don't understand. I have my own views in the matter.-- Besides, there's something else. You have been exceedingly indelicate. You took advantage of my ignorance. You let me think you were a rose-beetle and yesterday the snail told me you are a tumble-bug. A considerable difference! He saw you engaged in--well, doing something I don't care to mention. I'm sure you will now admit that I must take back my word."

Bobbie was stunned. When he recovered from the shock he burst out angrily:

"No, I *don't* understand. I can't understand. I want to be loved for myself, and not for my business."

"If only it weren't dung," said Effie offishly,

"anything but dung, I shouldn't be so particular.--
And please remember, I'm a young widow who lost
her husband only three days ago under the most
tragic circumstances--he was gobbled up by the
shrewmouse--and it isn't proper for me to be
gadding about. A young widow should lead a life of
complete retirement. So--good-by."

Pop into her hole went Effie, as though a puff of
wind had blown her away. Maya would never have
thought it possible that anyone could dive into the
ground as fast as that.

Effie was gone, and Bobbie stared in blank
bewilderment down the empty dark opening,
looking so utterly stupid that Maya had to laugh.

Finally he roused, and shook his small round head
in angry distress. His feelers drooped dismally like
two rain-soaked fans.

"People now-a-days no longer appreciate fineness
of character and respectability," he sighed. "Effie is
heartless. I didn't dare admit it to myself, but she is,
she's absolutely heartless. But even if she hasn't got
the *right feelings*, she ought to have the *good sense*
to be my wife."

Maya saw the tears come to his eyes, and her heart
was seized with pity.

But the next instant Bobbie stirred. He wiped the
tears away and crept cautiously behind a small
mound of earth, which his friend had probably
shoveled out of her dwelling. A little flesh-colored

earthworm was coming along through the grass. It had the queerest way of propelling itself, by first making itself long and thin, then short and thick. Its cylinder of a body consisted of nothing but delicate rings that pushed and groped forward noiselessly.

Suddenly, startling Maya, Bobbie made one step out of his hiding-place, caught hold of the worm, bit it in two, and began calmly to eat the one half, heedless of its desperate wriggling or the wriggling of the other half in the grass. It was a tiny little worm.

"Patience," said Bobbie, "it will soon be over."

But while he chewed, his thoughts seemed to revert to Effie, his Effie, whom he had lost forever and aye, and great tears rolled down his cheeks.

Maya pitied him from the bottom of her heart.

"Dear me," she thought, "there certainly is a lot of sadness in the world."

At that moment she saw the half of the worm which Bobbie had set aside, making a hasty departure.

"Did you *ever* see the like!" she cried, surprised into such a loud tone that Bobbie looked around wondering where the sound had come from.

"Make way!" he called.

"But I'm not in your way," said Maya.

"Where are you then? You must be somewhere."

"Up here. Up above you. In the bluebell."

"I believe you, but I'm no grasshopper. I can't turn my head up far enough to see you. Why did you scream?"

"The half of the worm is running away."

"Yes," said Bobbie, looking after the retreating fraction, "the creatures are very lively.-- I've lost my appetite." With that he threw away the remnant which he was still holding in his hand, and this worm portion also retreated, in the other direction.

Maya was completely puzzled. But Bobbie seemed to be familiar with this peculiarity of worms.

"Don't suppose that I always eat worms," he remarked. "You see, you don't find roses everywhere."

"Tell the little one at least which way its other half ran," cried Maya in great excitement.

Bobbie shook his head gravely.

"Those whom fate has rent asunder, let no man join together again," he observed.-- "Who are you?"

"Maya, of the nation of bees."

"I'm glad to hear it. I have nothing against the bees.-

- Why are you sitting about? Bees don't usually sit about. Have you been sitting there long?"

"I slept here."

"Indeed!" There was a note of suspicion in Bobbie's voice. "I hope you slept well, *very* well. Did you just wake up?"

"Yes," said Maya, who had shrewdly guessed that Bobbie would not like her having overheard his conversation with Effie, the cricket, and did not want to hurt his feelings again.

Bobbie ran hither and thither trying to look up and see Maya.

"Wait," he said. "If I raise myself on my hind legs and lean against that blade of grass I'll be able to see you, and you'll be able to look into my eyes. You want to, don't you?"

"Why, I do indeed. I'd like to very much."

Bobbie found a suitable prop, the stem of a buttercup. The flower tipped a little to one side so that Maya could see him perfectly as he raised himself on his hind legs and looked up at her. She thought he had a nice, dear, friendly face--but not so very young any more and cheeks rather too plump. He bowed, setting the buttercup a-rocking, and introduced himself:

"Bobbie, of the family of rose-beetles."

Maya had to laugh to herself. She knew very well he was not a rose-beetle; he was a dung-beetle. But she passed the matter over in silence, not caring to mortify him.

"Don't you mind the rain?" she asked.

"Oh, no. I'm accustomed to the rain--from the roses, you know. It's usually raining there."

Maya thought to herself:

"After all I must punish him a little for his brazen lies. He's so frightfully vain."

"Bobbie," she said with a sly smile, "what sort of a hole is that one there, under the leaf?"

Bobbie started.

"A hole? A hole, did you say? There are very many holes round here. It's probably just an ordinary hole. You have no idea how many holes there are in the ground."

Bobbie had hardly uttered the last word when something dreadful happened. In his eagerness to appear indifferent he had lost his balance and toppled over. Maya heard a despairing shriek, and the next instant saw the beetle lying flat on his back in the grass, his arms and legs waving pitifully in the air.

"I'm done for," he wailed, "I'm done for. I can't get

back on my feet again. I'll never be able to get back
on my feet again. I'll die. I'll die in this position.
Have you ever heard of a worse fate!"

He carried on so that he did not hear Maya trying to
comfort him. And he kept making efforts to touch
the ground with his feet. But each time he'd
painfully get hold of a bit of earth, it would give
way, and he'd fall over again on his high half-sphere
of a back. The case looked really desperate, and
Maya was honestly concerned; he was already quite
pale in the face and his cries were heart-rending.

"I can't stand it, I can't stand this position," he
yelled. "At least turn your head away. Don't torture
a dying man with your inquisitive stares.-- If only I
could reach a blade of grass, or the stem of the
buttercup. You can't hold on to the air. Nobody can
do that. Nobody can hold on to the air."

Maya's heart was quivering with pity.

"Wait," she cried, "I'll try to turn you over. If I try
very hard I am bound to succeed. But Bobbie,
Bobbie, dear man, don't yell like that. Listen to me.
If I bend a blade of grass over and reach the tip of it
to you, will you be able to use it and save yourself?"

Bobbie had no ears for her suggestion. Frightened
out of his senses, he did nothing but kick and
scream.

So little Maya, in spite of the rain, flew out of her
cover over to a slim green blade of grass beside
Bobbie, and clung to it near the tip. It bent under

her weight and sank directly above Bobbie's wriggling limbs. Maya gave a little cry of delight.

"Catch hold of it," she called.

Bobbie felt something tickle his face and quickly grabbed at it, first with one hand, then with the other, and finally with his legs, which had splendid sharp claws, two each. Bit by bit he drew himself along the blade until he reached the base, where it was thicker and stronger, and he was able to turn himself over on it.

He heaved a tremendous sigh of relief.

"Good God!" he exclaimed. "That was awful. But for my presence of mind I should have fallen a victim to your talkativeness."

"Are you feeling better?" asked Maya.

Bobbie clutched his forehead.

"Thanks, thanks. When this dizziness passes, I'll tell you all about it."

But Maya never got the answer to her question. A field-sparrow came hopping through the grass in search of insects, and the little bee pressed herself close to the ground and kept very quiet until the bird had gone. When she looked around for Bobbie he had disappeared. So she too made off; for the rain had stopped and the day was clear and warm.

CHAPTER V

THE ACROBAT

Oh, what a day!

The dew had fallen early in the morning, and when the sun rose and cast its slanting beams across the forest of grass, there was such a sparkling and glistening and gleaming that you didn't know what to say or do for sheer ecstasy, it was so beautiful, so beautiful!

The moment Maya awoke, glad sounds greeted her from all round. Some came out of the trees, from the throats of the birds, the dreaded creatures who could yet produce such exquisite song; other happy calls came out of the air, from flying insects, or out of the grass and the bushes, from bugs and flies, big ones and little ones.

Maya had made it very comfortable for herself in a hole in a tree. It was safe and dry, and stayed warm the greater part of the night because the sun shone on the entrance all day long. Once, early in the morning, she had heard a woodpecker rat-a-tat-tatting on the bark of the trunk, and had lost no time getting away. The drumming of a woodpecker is as terrifying to a little insect in the bark of a tree as the breaking open of our shutters by a burglar would be to us. But at night she was safe in her lofty nook. At night no creatures came prying.

She had sealed up part of the entrance with wax,

leaving just space enough to slip in and out; and in a cranny in the back of the hole, where it was dark and cool, she had stored a little honey against rainy days.

This morning she swung herself out into the sunshine with a cry of delight, all anticipation as to what the fresh, lovely day might bring. She sailed straight through the golden air, looking like a brisk dot driven by the wind.

"I am going to meet a human being to-day," she cried. "I feel sure I am. On days like this human beings must certainly be out in the open air enjoying nature."

Never had she met so many insects. There was a coming and going and all sorts of doings; the air was alive with a humming and a laughing and glad little cries. You had to join in, you just *had* to join in.

After a while Maya let herself down into a forest of grass, where all sorts of plants and flowers were growing. The highest were the white tufts of yarrow and butterfly-weed--the flaming milkweed that drew you like a magnet. She took a sip of nectar from some clover and was about to fly off again when she saw a perfect droll of a beast perched on a blade of grass curving above her flower. She was thoroughly scared--he was such a lean green monster--but then her interest was tremendously aroused, and she remained sitting still, as though rooted to the spot, and stared straight at him.

At first glance you'd have thought he had horns.
Looking closer you saw it was his oddly
protuberant forehead that gave this impression. Two
long, long feelers fine as the finest thread grew out
of his brows, and his body was the slimmest
imaginable, and green all over, even to his eyes. He
had dainty forelegs and thin, inconspicuous wings
that couldn't be very practical, Maya thought.
Oddest of all were his great hindlegs, which stuck
up over his body like two jointed stilts. His sly,
saucy expression was contradicted by the look of
astonishment in his eyes, and you couldn't say there
was any meanness in his eyes either. No, rather a lot
of good humor.

"Well, mademoiselle," he said to Maya, evidently
annoyed by her surprised expression, "never seen a
grasshopper before? Or are you laying eggs?"

"The idea!" cried Maya in shocked accents. "It
wouldn't occur to me. Even if I could, I wouldn't. It
would be usurping the sacred duties of our queen. I
wouldn't do such a foolish thing."

The grasshopper ducked his head and made such a
funny face that Maya had to laugh out loud in spite
of her chagrin.

"Mademoiselle," he began, then had to laugh
himself, and said: "You're a case! You're a case!"

The fellow's behavior made Maya impatient.

"Why do you laugh?" she asked in a not altogether
friendly tone. "You can't be serious expecting me to

lay eggs, especially out here on the grass."

There was a snap. "Hoppety-hop," said the grasshopper, and was gone.

Maya was utterly non-plussed. Without the help of his wings he had swung himself up in the air in a tremendous curve. Foolhardiness bordering on madness, she thought.

But there he was again. From where, she couldn't tell, but there he was, beside her, on a leaf of her clover.

He looked her up and down, all round, before and behind.

"No," he said then, pertly, "you certainly can't lay eggs. You're not equipped for it. You haven't got a borer."

"What--borer?" Maya covered herself with her wings and turned so that the stranger could see nothing but her face.

"Borer, that's what I said.-- Don't fall off your base, mademoiselle.-- You're a wasp, aren't you?"

To be called a wasp! Nothing worse could happen to little Maya.

"I *never*!" she cried.

"Hoppety-hop," answered he, and was off again.

"The fellow makes me nervous," she thought, and decided to fly away. She couldn't remember ever having been so insulted in her life. What a disgrace to be mistaken for a wasp, one of those useless wasps, those tramps, those common thieves! It really was infuriating.

But there he was again!

"Mademoiselle," he called and turned round part way, so that his long hindlegs looked like the hands of a clock standing at five minutes before half-past seven, "mademoiselle, you must excuse me for interrupting our conversation now and then. But suddenly I'm seized. I must hop. I can't help it, I must hop, no matter where. Can't you hop, too?"

He smiled a smile that drew his mouth from ear to ear. Maya couldn't keep from laughing.

"Can you?" said the grasshopper, and nodded encouragingly.

"Who *are* you?" asked Maya. "You're terribly exciting."

"Why, everybody knows who I am," said the green oddity, and grinned almost beyond the limits of his jaws.

Maya never could make out whether he spoke in fun or in earnest.

"I'm a stranger in these parts," she replied

pleasantly, "else I'm sure I'd know you.-- But please note that I belong to the family of bees, and am positively not a wasp."

"My goodness," said the grasshopper, "one and the same thing."

Maya couldn't utter a sound, she was so excited.

"You're uneducated," she burst out at length. "Take a good look at a wasp once."

"Why should I?" answered the green one. "What good would it do if I observed differences that exist only in people's imagination? You, a bee, fly round in the air, sting everything you come across, and can't hop. Exactly the same with a wasp. So where's the difference? Hoppety-hop!" And he was gone.

"But now I am going to fly away," thought Maya.

There he was again.

"Mademoiselle," he called, "there's going to be a hopping-match to-morrow. It will be held in the Reverend Sinpeck's garden. Would you care to have a complimentary ticket and watch the games? My old woman has two left over. She'll trade you one for a compliment. I expect to break the record."

"I'm not interested in hopping acrobatics," said Maya in some disgust. "A person who flies has *higher* interests."

The grasshopper grinned a grin you could almost hear.

"Don't think *too* highly of yourself, my dear young lady. Most creatures in this world can fly, but only a very, very few can hop. You don't understand other people's interests. You have no vision. Even human beings would like a high elegant hop. The other day I saw the Reverend Sinpeck hop a yard up into the air to impress a little snake that slid across his road. His contempt for anything that couldn't hop was so great that he threw away his pipe. And reverends, you know, cannot live without their pipes. I have known grasshoppers--members of my own family-- who could hop to a height three hundred times their length. *Now* you're impressed. You haven't a word to say. And you're inwardly regretting the remarks you made and the remarks you intended to make. Three hundred times their own length! Just imagine. Even the elephant, the largest animal in the world, can't hop as high as that. Well? You're not saying anything. Didn't I tell you you wouldn't have anything to say?"

"But how *can* I say anything if you don't give me a chance?"

"All right, then, talk," said the grasshopper pleasantly. "Hoppety-hop." He was gone.

Maya had to laugh in spite of her irritation.

The fellow had certainly furnished her with a strange experience. Buffoon though he was, still she had to admire his wide information and worldly wisdom; and though she could not agree with his views of hopping, she was amazed by all the new things he had taught her in their brief conversation. If he had been more reliable she would have been only too glad to ask him questions about a number of different things. It occurred to her that often people who are least equipped to profit by experiences are the very ones who have them.

He knew the names of human beings. Did he, then, understand their language? If he came back, she'd ask him. And she'd also ask him what he thought of trying to go near a human being or of entering a human being's house.

"Mademoiselle!" A blade of grass beside Maya was set swaying.

"Goodness gracious! Where do you keep coming from?"

"The surroundings."

"But do tell, do you hop out into the world just so, without knowing where you mean to land?"

"Of course. Why not? Can *you* read the future? No one can. Only the tree-toad, but he never tells."

"The things you know! Wonderful, simply wonderful!-- Do you understand the language of human beings?"

"That's a difficult question to answer,

mademoiselle, because it hasn't been proved as yet whether human beings have a language. Sometimes they utter sounds by which they seem to reach an understanding with each other--but such awful sounds! So unmelodious! Like nothing else in nature that I know of. However, there's one thing you must allow them: they do seem to try to make their voices pleasanter. Once I saw two boys take a blade of grass between their thumbs and blow on it. The result was a whistle which may be compared with the chirping of a cricket, though far inferior in quality of tone, far inferior. However, human beings make an honest effort.-- Is there anything else you'd like to ask? I know a thing or two."

He grinned his almost-audible grin.

But the next time he hopped off, Maya waited for him in vain. She looked about in the grass and the flowers; he was nowhere to be seen.

CHAPTER VI

PUCK

Maya, drowsy with the noonday heat, flew leisurely past the glare on the bushes in the garden, into the cool, broad-leaved shelter of a great chestnut-tree.

On the trodden sward in the shade under the tree stood chairs and tables, evidently for an out-door meal. A short distance away gleamed the red-tiled roof of a peasant's cottage, with thin blue columns of smoke curling up from the chimneys.

Now at last, thought Maya, she was bound to see a human being. Had she not reached the very heart of his realm? The tree must be his property, and the curious wooden contrivances in the shade below must belong to his hive.

Something buzzed; a fly alighted on the leaf beside her. It ran up and down the green veining in little jerks. You couldn't see its legs move, and it seemed to be sliding about excitedly. Then it flew from one finger of the broad leaf to another, but so quickly and unexpectedly that you might have thought it hadn't flown but hopped. Evidently it was looking for the most comfortable place on the leaf. Every now and then, in the suddennest way, it would swing itself up in the air a short space and buzz vehemently, as though something dreadfully untoward had occurred, or as though it were animated by some tremendous purpose. Then it would drop back to the leaf, as if nothing had happened, and resume its jerky racing up and down. Lastly, it would sit quite still, like a rigid image.

Maya watched its antics in the sunshine, then approached it and said politely:

"How do you do? Welcome to my leaf. You are a fly, are you not?"

"What else do you take me for?" said the little one. "My name is Puck. I am very busy. Do you want to drive me away?"

"Why, not at all. I am glad to make your acquaintance."

"I believe you," was all Puck said, and with that he tried to pull his head off.

"Mercy!" cried Maya.

"I must do this. You don't understand. It's something you know nothing about," Puck rejoined calmly, and slid his legs over his wings till they curved round the tip of his body. "I'm more than a fly," he added with some pride. "I'm a housefly. I flew out here for the fresh air."

"How interesting!" exclaimed Maya gleefully. "Then you must know all about human beings."

"As well as the pockets of my trousers," Puck threw out disdainfully. "I sit on them every day. Didn't you know *that*? I thought you bees were so *clever*. You pretend to be at any rate."

"My name is Maya," said the little bee rather shyly. Where the other insects got their self-assurance, to say nothing of their insolence, she couldn't understand.

"Thanks for the information. Whatever your name, you're a simpleton."

Puck sat there tilted like a cannon in position to be fired off, his head and breast thrust upward, the hind tip of his body resting on the leaf. Suddenly he ducked his head and squatted down, so that he looked as if he had no legs.

"You've got to watch out and be careful," he said. "That's the most important thing of all."

But an angry wave of resentment was surging in little Maya. The insult Puck had offered her was too much. Without really knowing what made her do it, she pounced on him quick as lightning, caught him by the collar and held him tight.

"I will teach you to be polite to a bee," she cried.

Puck set up an awful howl.

"Don't sting me," he screamed. "It's the only thing you can do, but it's killing. Please remove the back of your body. That's where your sting is. And let me go, please let me go, if you possibly can. I'll do anything you say. Can't you understand a joke, a mere joke? Everybody knows that you bees are the most respected of all insects, and the most powerful, and the most numerous. Only don't kill me, please don't. There won't be any bringing me back to life. Good God! No one appreciates my humor!"

"Very well," said Maya with a touch of contempt in her heart, "I'll let you live on condition that you tell me everything you know about human beings."

"Gladly," cried Puck. "I'd have told you anyhow. But please let me go now."

Maya released him. She had stopped caring. Her respect for the fly and any confidence she might have had in him were gone. Of what value could the experiences of so low, so vulgar a creature be to serious-minded people? She would have to find out about human beings for herself.

The lesson, however, had not been wasted. Puck was much more endurable now. Scolding and growling he set himself to rights. He smoothed down his feelers and wings and the minute hairs on his black body--which were fearfully rumpled; for the girl-bee had laid on good and hard--and concluded the operation by running his proboscis in and out several times--something new to Maya.

"Out of joint, completely out of joint!" he muttered in a pained tone. "Comes of your excited way of doing things. Look. See for yourself. The sucking-disk at the end of my proboscis looks like a twisted pewter plate."

"Have you a sucking-disk?" asked Maya.

"Goodness gracious, of course!-- Now tell me. What do you want to know about human beings?-- Never mind about my proboscis being out of joint. It'll be all right.-- I think I had best tell you a few things from my own life. You see, I grew up among human beings, so you'll hear just what you want to know."

"You grew up among human beings?"

"Of course. It was in the corner of their room that

my mother laid the egg from which I came. I made
my first attempts to walk on their window-shades,
and I tested the strength of my wings by flying from
Schiller to Goethe."

"What are Schiller and Goethe?"

"Statues," explained Puck, very superior, "statues of
two men who seem to have distinguished
themselves. They stand under the mirror, one on the
right hand and one on the left hand, and nobody
pays any attention to them."

"What's a mirror? And why do the statues stand
under the mirror?"

"A mirror is good for seeing your belly when you
crawl on it. It's very amusing. When human beings
go up to a mirror, they either put their hands up to
their hair, or pull at their beards. When they are
alone, they smile into the mirror, but if somebody
else is in the room they look very serious. What the
purpose of it is, I could never make out. Seems to
be some useless game of theirs. I myself, when I
was still a child, suffered a good deal from the
mirror. I'd fly into it and of course be thrown back
violently."

Maya plied Puck with more questions about the
mirror, which he found very difficult to answer.

"Here," he said at last, "you've certainly flown over
the smooth surface of water, haven't you? Well, a
mirror is something like it, only hard and upright."

The little fly, seeing that Maya listened most respectfully and attentively to the tale of his experiences, became a good deal pleasanter in his manners. And as for Maya's opinion of Puck, although she didn't believe everything he told her, still she was sorry she had thought so slightingly of him earlier in their meeting.

"Often people are far more sensible than we take them to be at first," she told herself.

Puck went on with his story.

"It took a long time for me to get to understand their language. Now at last I know what they want. It isn't much, because they usually say the same thing every day."

"I can scarcely believe it," said Maya. "Why, they have so many interests, and think so many things, and do so many things. Cassandra told me that they build cities so big that you can't fly round them in one day, towers as high as the nuptial flight of our queen, houses that float on the water, and houses that glide across the country on two narrow silver paths and go faster than birds."

"Wait a moment!" said Puck energetically. "Who is Cassandra? Who is she, if I may make so bold as to ask? Well?"

"Oh, she was my teacher."

"Teacher!" repeated Puck contemptuously. "Probably also a bee. Who but a bee would overestimate human beings like that? Your Miss Cassandra, or whatever her name is, doesn't know her history. Those cities and towers and other human devices you speak of are none of them any good to us. Who would take such an impractical view of the world as you do? If you don't accept the premise that the earth is dominated by the flies, that the flies are the most widespread and most important race on earth, you'll scarcely get a real knowledge of the world."

Puck took a few excited zigzag turns on the leaf and pulled at his head, to Maya's intense concern. However, the little bee had observed by this time that there wasn't much sense to be got out of his head any way.

"Do you know how you can tell I am right?" asked Puck, rubbing his hands together as if to tie them in a knot. "Count the number of people and the number of flies in any room. The result will surprise you."

"You may be right. But that's not the point."

"Do you think I was born this year?" Puck demanded all of a sudden.

"I don't know."

"I passed through a winter," Puck announced, all pride. "My experiences date back to the ice age. In a sense they take me *through* the ice age. That's why I'm here--I'm here to recuperate."

"Whatever else you may be, you certainly are spunky," remarked Maya.

"I should say so," exclaimed Puck, and made an airy leap out into the sunshine. "The flies are the boldest race in creation. We never run away unless it is better to run away, and then we always come back.-- Have you ever sat on a human being?"

"No," said Maya, looking at the fly distrustfully out of the corner of her eye. She still didn't know quite what to make of him. "No, I'm not interested in sitting on human beings."

"Ah, dear child, that's because you don't know what it is. If ever you had seen the fun I have with the man at home, you'd turn green with envy. I'll tell you.-- In my room there lives an elderly man who cherishes the color of his nose by means of a peculiar drink, which he keeps hidden in the corner cupboard. It has a sweet, intoxicating smell. When he goes to get it he smiles, and his eyes grow small. He takes a little glass, and he looks up to the ceiling while he drinks, to see if I am there. I nod down to him, and he passes his hand over his forehead, nose and mouth to show me where I am to sit later on. Then he blinks, and opens his mouth as wide as he can, and pulls down the shade to keep the afternoon sun from bothering us. Finally he lays himself down on a something called a sofa, and in a short while begins to make dull snuffling sounds. I suppose he thinks the sounds are beautiful. We'll talk about them some other time. They are man's slumber song. For me they are the sign that I am to come down. The first thing I do is to take my portion from the glass, which he left for me. There's something tremendously stimulating about a drop like that. I understand human beings. Then I fly over and take my place on the forehead of the sleeping man. The forehead lies between the nose and the hair and serves for thinking. You can tell it does from the long furrows that go from right to left. They must move whenever a man thinks if something worth while is to result from his thinking. The forehead also shows if human beings are annoyed. But then the folds run up and down, and a round cavity forms over the nose. As soon as I settle on his forehead and begin to run to and fro in the furrows, the man makes a snatch in the air with his hands. He thinks I'm somewhere in the air. That's because I'm sitting on his think-furrows, and he can't work out so quickly where I really am. At last he does. He mutters and jabs at me. Now then, Miss Maya, or whatever your name is, now then, you've got to have your wits about you. I see the hand coming, but I wait until the last moment, then I fly nimbly to one side, sit down, and watch him feel to see if I am still there.-- We kept the game up often for a full half hour. You have no idea what a lot of endurance the man has. Finally he jumps up and pours out a string of words which show how ungrateful he is. Well, what of it? A noble soul seeks no reward. I'm already up on the ceiling listening to his ungrateful outburst."

"I can't say I particularly like it," observed Maya. "Isn't it rather useless?"

"Do you expect me to erect a honeycomb on his nose?" exclaimed Puck. "You have no sense of humor, dear girl. What do *you* do that's useful?"

Little Maya went red all over, but quickly collected herself to hide her embarrassment from Puck.

"The time is coming," she flashed, "when I shall do something big and splendid, and good and useful too. But first I want to see what is going on in the world. Deep down in my heart I feel that the time is coming."

As Maya spoke she felt a hot tide of hope and enthusiasm flood her being.

Puck seemed not to realize how serious she was, and how deeply stirred. He zigzagged about in his flurried way for a while, then asked:

"You don't happen to have any honey with you, do you, my dear?"

"I'm so sorry," replied Maya. "I'd gladly let you have some, especially after you've entertained me so pleasantly, but I really haven't got any with me.-- May I ask you one more question?"

"Shoot," said Puck. "I'll answer, I'll always answer."

"I'd like to know how I could get into a human being's house."

"Fly in," said Puck sagaciously.

"But how, without running into danger?"

"Wait until a window is opened. But be sure to find the way out again. Once you're inside, if you can't find the window, the best thing to do is to fly toward the light. You'll always find plenty of windows in every house. You need only notice where the sun shines through. Are you going already?"

"Yes," replied Maya, holding out her hand. "I have some things to attend to. Good-by. I hope you quite recover from the effects of the ice age."

And with her fine confident buzz that yet sounded slightly anxious, little Maya raised her gleaming wings and flew out into the sunshine across to the flowery meadows to cull a little nourishment.

Puck looked after her, and carefully meditated what might still be said. Then he observed thoughtfully:

"Well, now. Well, well.-- Why not?"

CHAPTER VII

IN THE TOILS

After her meeting with Puck the fly Maya was not in a particularly happy frame of mind. She could not bring herself to believe that he was right in everything he had said about human beings, or right in his relations to them. She had formed an entirely different conception--a much finer, lovelier picture, and she fought against letting her mind harbor low or ridiculous ideas of mankind. Yet she was still afraid to enter a human dwelling. How was she to know whether or not the owner would like it? And she wouldn't for all the world make herself a burden to anyone.

Her thoughts went back once more to the things Cassandra had told her.

"They are good and wise," Cassandra had said. "They are strong and powerful, but they never abuse their power. On the contrary, wherever they go they bring order and prosperity. We bees, knowing they are friendly to us, put ourselves under their protection and share our honey with them. They leave us enough for the winter, they provide us with shelter against the cold, and guard us against the hosts of our enemies among the animals. There are few creatures in the world who have entered into such a relation of friendship and voluntary service with human beings. Among the insects you will often hear voices raised to speak evil of man. Don't listen to them. If a foolish tribe of bees ever returns to the wild and tries to do without human beings, it soon perishes. There are too many beasts that hanker for our honey, and often a whole bee-city-- all its buildings, all its inhabitants--has been ruthlessly destroyed, merely because a senseless animal wanted to satisfy its greed for honey."

That is what Cassandra had told Maya about human beings, and until Maya had convinced herself of the contrary, she wanted to keep this belief in them.

It was now afternoon. The sun was dropping behind

the fruit trees in a large vegetable garden through which Maya was flying. The trees were long past flowering, but the little bee still remembered them in the shining glory of countless blossoms, whiter than light, lovely, pure, and exquisite against the blue of the heavens. The delicious perfume, the gleam and the shimmer--oh, she'd never forget the rapture of it as long as she lived.

As she flew she thought of how all that beauty would come again, and her heart expanded with delight in the glory of the great world in which she was permitted to live.

At the end of the garden shone the starry tufts of the jasmine--delicate yellow faces set in a wreath of pure white--sweet perfume wafted to Maya on the soft wings of the breeze.

And weren't there still some trees in bloom? Wasn't it the season for lindens? Maya thought delightedly of the big serious lindens, whose tops held the red glow of the setting sun to the very last.

She flew in among the stems of the blackberry vines, which were putting forth green berries and yielding blossoms at the same time. As she mounted again to reach the jasmine, something strange to the touch suddenly laid itself across her forehead and shoulders, and just as quickly covered her wings. It was the queerest sensation, as if her wings were crippled and she were suddenly restrained in her flight, and were falling, helplessly falling. A secret, wicked force seemed to be holding her feelers, her legs, her wings in invisible captivity. But she did

not fall. Though she could no longer move her
wings, she still hung in the air rocking, caught by a
marvelously yielding softness and delicacy, raised a
little, lowered a little, tossed here, tossed there, like
a loose leaf in a faint breeze.

Maya was troubled, but not as yet actually terrified.
Why should she be? There was no pain nor real
discomfort of any sort. Simply that it was so
peculiar, so very peculiar, and something bad
seemed to be lurking in the background. She must
get on. If she tried very hard, she could, assuredly.

But now she saw a thread across her breast, an
elastic silvery thread finer than the finest silk. She
clutched at it quickly, in a cold wave of terror. It
clung to her hand; it wouldn't shake off. And there
ran another silver thread over her shoulders. It drew
itself across her wings and tied them together--her
wings were powerless. And there, and there!
Everywhere in the air and above her body--those
bright, glittering, gluey threads!

Maya screamed with horror. Now she knew! Oh--
oh, now she knew! She was in a spider's web.

Her terrified shrieks rang out in the silent dome of
the summer day, where the sunshine touched the
green of the leaves into gold, and insects flitted to
and fro, and birds swooped gaily from tree to tree.
Nearby, the jasmine sent its perfume into the air--
the jasmine she had wanted to reach. Now all was
over.

A small bluish butterfly, with brown dots gleaming

like copper on its wings, came flying very close.

"Oh, you poor soul," it cried, hearing Maya's screams and seeing her desperate plight. "May your death be an easy one, lovely child. I cannot help you. Some day, perhaps this very night, I shall meet with the same fate. But meanwhile life is still lovely for me. Good-by. Don't forget the sunshine in the deep sleep of death."

And the blue butterfly rocked away, drugged by the sunshine and the flowers and its own joy of living.

The tears streamed from Maya's eyes; she lost her last shred of self-control. She tossed her captive body to and fro, and buzzed as loud as she could, and screamed for help--from whom she did not know. But the more she tossed the tighter she enmeshed herself in the web. Now, in her great agony, Cassandra's warnings went through her mind:

"Beware of the spider and its web. If we bees fall into the spider's power we suffer the most gruesome death. The spider is heartless and tricky, and once it has a person in its toils, it never lets him go."

In a great flare of mortal terror Maya made one huge desperate effort. Somewhere one of the long, heavier suspension threads snapped. Maya felt it break, yet at the same time she sensed the awful doom of the cobweb. This was, that the more one struggled in it, the more effectively and dangerously it worked. She gave up, in complete exhaustion.

At that moment she saw the spider herself--very near, under a blackberry leaf. At sight of the great monster, silent and serious, crouching there as if ready to pounce, Maya's horror was indescribable. The wicked shining eyes were fastened on the little bee in sinister, cold-blooded patience.

Maya gave one loud shriek. This was the worst agony of all. Death itself could look no worse than that grey, hairy monster with her mean fangs and the raised legs supporting her fat body like a scaffolding. She would come rushing upon her, and then all would be over.

Now a dreadful fury of anger came upon Maya, such as she had never felt before. Forgetting her great agony, intent only upon one thing--selling her life as dearly as possible--she uttered her clear, alarming battle-cry, which all beasts knew and dreaded.

"You will pay for your cunning with death," she shouted at the spider. "Just come and try to kill me, you'll find out what a bee can do."

The spider did not budge. She really was uncanny and must have terrified bigger creatures than little Maya.

Strong in her anger, Maya now made another violent, desperate effort. Snap! One of the long suspension threads above her broke. The web was probably meant for flies and gnats, not for such large insects as bees.

But Maya got herself only more entangled.

In one gliding motion the spider drew quite close to Maya. She swung by her nimble legs upon a single thread with her body hanging straight downward.

"What right have you to break my net?" she rasped at Maya. "What are you doing here? Isn't the world big enough for you? Why do you disturb a peaceful recluse?"

That was not what Maya had expected to hear. Most certainly not.

"I didn't mean to," she cried, quivering with glad hope. Ugly as the spider was, still she did not seem to intend any harm. "I didn't see your web and I got tangled in it. I'm so sorry. Please pardon me."

The spider drew nearer.

"You're a funny little body," she said, letting go of the thread first with one leg, then with the other. The delicate thread shook. How wonderful that it could support the great creature.

"Oh, do help me out of this," begged Maya, "I should be so grateful."

"That's what I came here for," said the spider, and smiled strangely. For all her smiling she looked mean and deceitful. "Your tossing and tugging spoils the whole web. Keep quiet one second, and I will set you free."

"Oh, thanks! Ever so many thanks!" cried Maya.

The spider was now right beside her. She examined the web carefully to see how securely Maya was entangled.

"How about your sting?" she asked.

Ugh, how mean and horrid she looked! Maya fairly shivered with disgust at the thought that she was going to touch her, but replied as pleasantly as she could:

"Don't trouble about my sting. I will draw it in, and nobody can hurt himself on it then."

"I should hope not," said the spider. "Now, then, look out! Keep quiet. Too bad for my web."

Maya remained still. Suddenly she felt herself being whirled round and round on the same spot, till she got dizzy and sick and had to close her eyes.-- But what was that? She opened her eyes quickly. Horrors! She was completely enmeshed in a fresh sticky thread which the spider must have had with her.

"My God!" cried little Maya softly, in a quivering voice. That was all she said. Now she saw how tricky the spider had been; now she was really caught beyond release; now there was absolutely no chance of escape. She could no longer move any part of her body. The end was near.

Her fury of anger was gone, there was only a great sadness in her heart.

"I didn't know there was such meanness and wickedness in the world," she thought. "The deep night of death is upon me. Good-by, dear bright sun. Good-by, my dear friend-bees. Why did I leave you? A happy life to you. I must die."

The spider sat wary, a little to one side. She was still afraid of Maya's sting.

"Well?" she jeered. "How are you feeling, little girl?"

Maya was too proud to answer the false creature. She merely said, after a while when she felt she couldn't bear any more:

"Please kill me right away."

"Really!" said the spider, tying a few torn threads together. "Really! Do you take me to be as big a dunce as yourself? You're going to die anyhow, if you're kept hanging long enough, and that's the time for me to suck the blood out of you--when you can't sting. Too bad, though, that you can't see how dreadfully you've damaged my lovely web. Then you'd realize that you deserve to die."

She dropped down to the ground, laid the end of the newly spun thread about a stone, and pulled it in tight. Then she ran up again, caught hold of the thread by which little enmeshed Maya hung, and dragged her captive along.

"You're going into the shade, my dear," she said, "so that you shall not dry up out here in the sunshine. Besides, hanging here you're like a scarecrow, you'll frighten away other nice little mortals who don't watch where they're going. And sometimes the sparrows come and rob my web.-- To let you know with whom you're dealing, my name is Thekla, of the family of cross-spiders. You needn't tell me your name. It makes no difference. You're a fat bit, and you'll taste just as tender and juicy by any name."

So little Maya hung in the shade of the blackberry vine, close to the ground, completely at the mercy of the cruel spider, who intended her to die by slow starvation. Hanging with her little head downward-- a fearful position to be in--she soon felt she would not last many more minutes. She whimpered softly, and her cries for help grew feebler and feebler. Who was there to hear? Her folk at home knew nothing of this catastrophe, so *they* couldn't come hurrying to her rescue.

Suddenly down, in the grass, she heard some one growling:

"Make way! *I'm* coming."

Maya's agonized heart began to beat stormily. She recognized the voice of Bobbie, the dung-beetle.

"Bobbie," she called, as loud as she could, "Bobbie, dear Bobbie!"

"Make way! *I'm* coming."

"But I'm not in your way, Bobbie," cried Maya. "Oh dear, I'm hanging over your head. The spider has caught me."

"Who are you?" asked Bobbie. "So many people know me. You know they do, don't you?"

"I am Maya--Maya, the bee. Oh please, please help me!"

"Maya? Maya?-- Ah, now I remember. You made my acquaintance several weeks ago.-- The deuce! You *are* in a bad way, if I must say so myself. You certainly do need my help. As I happen to have a few moments' time, I won't refuse."

"Oh, Bobbie, can you tear these threads?"

"Tear those threads! Do you mean to insult me?" Bobbie slapped the muscles of his arm. "Look, little girl. Hard as steel. No match for *that* in strength. I can do more than smash a few cobwebs. You'll see something that'll make you open your eyes."

Bobbie crawled up on the leaf, caught hold of the thread by which Maya was hanging, clung to it, then let go of the leaf. The thread broke, and they both fell to the ground.

"That's only the beginning," said Bobbie.-- "But Maya, you're trembling. My dear child, you poor little girl, how pale you are! Now who would be so afraid of death? You must look death calmly in the face as I do. So. I'll unwrap you now."

Maya could not utter a syllable. Bright tears of joy ran down her cheeks. She was to be free again, fly again in the sunshine, wherever she wished. She was to live.

But then she saw the spider coming down the blackberry vine.

"Bobbie," she screamed, "the spider's coming."

Bobbie went on unperturbed, merely laughing to himself. He really was an extraordinarily strong insect.

"She'll think twice before she comes nearer," he said.

But there! The vile voice rasped above them:

"Robbers! Help! I'm being robbed. You fat lump, what are you doing with my prey?"

"Don't excite yourself, madam," said Bobbie. "I have a right, haven't I, to talk to my friend. If you say another word to displease me, I'll tear your whole web to shreds. Well? Why so silent all of a sudden?"

"I am defeated," said the spider.

"That has nothing to do with the case," observed Bobbie. "Now you'd better be getting away from here."

The spider cast a look at Bobbie full of hate and venom; but glancing up at her web she reconsidered, and turned away slowly, furious, scolding and growling under her breath. Fangs and stings were of no avail. They wouldn't even leave a mark on armor such as Bobbie wore. With violent denunciations against the injustice in the world, the spider hid herself away inside a withered leaf, from which she could spy out and watch over her web.

Meanwhile Bobbie finished the unwrapping of Maya. He tore the network and released her legs and wings. The rest she could do herself. She preened herself happily. But she had to go slow, because she was still weak from fright.

"You must forget what you have been through," said Bobbie. "Then you'll stop trembling. Now see if you can fly. Try."

Maya lifted herself with a little buzz. Her wings worked splendidly, and to her intense joy she felt that no part of her body had been injured. She flew slowly up to the jasmine flowers, drank avidly of their abundant scented honey-juice, and returned to Bobbie, who had left the blackberry vines and was sitting in the grass.

"I thank you with my whole heart and soul," said Maya, deeply moved and happy in her regained freedom.

"Thanks are in place," observed Bobbie. "But that's the way I always am--always doing something for other people. Now fly away. I'd advise you to lay

your head on your pillow early to-night. Have you
far to go?"

"No," said Maya. "Only a short way. I live at the
edge of the beech-woods. Good-by, Bobbie, I'll
never forget you, never, never, so long as I live.
Good-by."

CHAPTER VIII

THE BUG AND THE BUTTERFLY

Her adventure with the spider gave Maya something
to think about. She made up her mind to be more
cautious in the future, not to rush into things so
recklessly. Cassandra's prudent warnings about the
greatest dangers that threaten the bees, were enough
to give one pause; and there were all sorts of other
possibilities, and the world was such a big place--
oh, there was a good deal to make a little bee stop
and think.

It was in the evening particularly, when twilight fell
and the little bee was all by herself, that one
consideration after another stirred her mind. But the
next morning, if the sun shone, she usually forgot
half the things that had bothered her the night
before, and allowed her eagerness for experiences
to drive her out again into the gay whirl of life.

One day she met a very curious creature. It was
angular and flat as a pancake, but had a rather neat
design on its sheath; and whether its sheath were

wings or what, you couldn't really tell. The odd
little monster sat absolutely still on the shaded leaf
of a raspberry bush, its eyes half closed, apparently
sunk in meditation. The scent of the raspberries
spread around it deliciously. Maya wanted to find
out what sort of an animal it was. She flew to the
next-door leaf and said how-do-you-do. The
stranger made no reply.

"How do you do, again?" And Maya gave its leaf a
little tap. The flat object peeled one eye open,
turned it on Maya, and said:

"A bee. The world is full of bees," and closed its
eye again.

"Unique," thought Maya, and determined to get at
the stranger's secret. For now it excited her curiosity
more than ever, as people often do who pay no
attention to us. She tried honey. "I have plenty of
honey," she said. "May I offer you some?" The
stranger opened its one eye and regarded Maya
contemplatively a moment or two. "What is it going
to say this time?" Maya wondered.

This time there was no answer at all. The one eye
merely closed again, and the stranger sat quite still,
tight on the leaf, so that you couldn't see its legs and
you'd have thought it had been pressed down flat
with a thumb.

Maya realized, of course, that the stranger wanted
to ignore her, but--you know how it is--you don't
like being snubbed, especially if you haven't found
out what you wanted to find out. It makes you feel

so cheap.

"Whoever you are," cried Maya, "permit me to
inform you that insects are in the habit of greeting
each other, especially when one of them happens to
be a bee." The bug sat on without budging. It did
not so much as open its one eye again. "It's ill,"
thought Maya. "How horrid to be ill on a lovely day
like this. That's why it's staying in the shade, too."
She flew over to the bug's leaf and sat down beside
it. "Aren't you feeling well?" she asked, so very
friendly.

At this the funny creature began to move away.
"Move" is the only word to use, because it didn't
walk, or run, or fly, or hop. It went as if shoved by
an invisible hand.

"It hasn't any legs. That's why it's so cross," thought
Maya.

When it reached the stem of the leaf it stopped a
second, moved on again, and, to her astonishment,
Maya saw that it had left behind a little brown drop.

"How *very* singular," she thought--and clapped her
hand to her nose and held it tight shut. The veriest
stench came from the little brown drop. Maya
almost fainted. She flew away as fast as she could
and seated herself on a raspberry, where she held on
to her nose and shivered with disgust and
excitement.

"Serves you right," someone above her called, and
laughed. "Why take up with a stink-bug?"

"Don't laugh!" cried Maya.

She looked up. A white butterfly had alighted overhead on a slender, swaying branch of the raspberry bush, and was slowly opening and closing its broad wings--slowly, softly, silently, happy in the sunshine--black corners to its wings, round black marks in the centre of each wing, four round black marks in all. Ah, how beautiful, how beautiful! Maya forgot her vexation. And she was glad, too, to talk to the butterfly. She had never made the acquaintance of one before even though she had met a great many.

"Oh," she said, "you probably are right to laugh. Was that a stink-bug?"

"It was," he replied, still smiling. "The sort of person to keep away from. You're probably very young still?"

"Well," observed Maya, "I shouldn't say I was-- exactly. I've been through a great deal. But that was the first specimen of the kind I had ever come across. Can you imagine doing such a thing?"

The butterfly had to laugh again.

"You see," he explained, "stink-bugs like to keep to themselves. They are not very popular, so they use the odoriferous drop to make people take notice of them. We'd probably soon forget the fact of their existence if it were not for the drop: it serves as a reminder. And they want to be remembered, no matter how."

"How lovely, how exquisitely lovely your wings are," said Maya. "So delicate and white. May I introduce myself? Maya, of the nation of bees."

The butterfly laid his wings together to look like only one wing standing straight up in the air. He gave a slight bow.

"Fred," he said laconically.

Maya couldn't gaze her fill.

"Fly a little," she asked.

"Shall I fly away?"

"Oh no. I just want to see your great white wings move in the blue air. But never mind. I can wait till later. Where do you live?"

"Nowhere specially. A settled home is too much of a nuisance. Life didn't get to be really delightful until I turned into a butterfly. Before that, while I was still a caterpillar, I couldn't leave the cabbage the livelong day, and all one did was eat and squabble."

"Just what do you mean?" asked Maya, mystified.

"I used to be a caterpillar," explained Fred.

"Never!" cried Maya.

"Now, now, now," said Fred, pointing both feelers

straight at Maya. "Everyone knows a butterfly is first a caterpillar. Even human beings know it."

Maya was utterly perplexed. Could such a thing be?

"You must really explain more clearly," she said. "I couldn't accept what you say just so, could I? You wouldn't expect me to."

The butterfly perched beside the little bee on the slender swaying branch of the raspberry bush, and they rocked together in the morning wind. He told her how he had begun life as a caterpillar and then, one day, when he had shed his last caterpillar skin, he came out a pupa or chrysalis.

"At the end of a few weeks," he continued, "I woke up out of my dark sleep and broke through the wrappings or pupa-case. I can't tell you, Maya, what a feeling comes over you when, after a time like that, you suddenly see the sun again. I felt as though I were melting in a warm golden ocean, and I loved my life so that my heart began to pound."

"I understand," said Maya, "I understand. I felt the same way the first time I left our humdrum city and flew out into the bright scented world of blossoms." The little bee was silent a while, thinking of her first flight.-- But then she wanted to know how the butterfly's large wings could grow in the small space of the pupa-case.

Fred explained.

"The wings are delicately folded together like the

petals of a flower in the bud. When the weather is bright and warm, the flower must open, it cannot help itself, and its petals unfold. So with my wings, they were folded up, then unfolded. No one can resist the sun when it shines."

"No, no--one cannot--one cannot resist the sunshine." Maya mused, watching the butterfly as he perched in the golden light of the morning, pure white against the blue sky.

"People often charge us with being frivolous," said Fred. "We're really happy--just that--just happy. You wouldn't believe how seriously I sometimes think about life."

"Tell me what all you think."

"Oh," said Fred, "I think about the future. It's very interesting to think about the future.-- But I should like to fly now. The meadows on the hillside are full of yarrow and canterbury bells; everything's in bloom. I'd like to be there, you know."

This Maya understood, she understood it well, and they said good-by and flew away in different directions, the white butterfly rocking silently as if wafted by the gentle wind, little Maya with that uneasy zoom-zoom of the bees which we hear upon the flowers on fair days and which we always recall when we think of the summer.

CHAPTER IX

THE LOST LEG

Near the hole where Maya had set herself up for the summer lived a family of bark-boring beetles. Fridolin, the father, was an earnest, industrious man who wanted many children and took immense pains to bring up a large family. He had done very well: he had fifty energetic sons to fill him with pride and high hopes. Each had dug his own meandering little tunnel in the bark of the pine-tree and all were getting on and were comfortably settled.

"My wife," Fridolin said to Maya, after they had known each other some time, "has arranged things so that none of my sons interferes with the others. They are not even acquainted; each goes his own way."

Maya knew that human beings were none too fond of Fridolin and his people, though she herself liked him and liked his opinions and had found no reason to avoid him. In the morning before the sun arose and the woods were still asleep, she would hear his fine tapping and boring. It sounded like a delicate trickling, or as if the tree were breathing in its sleep. Later she would see the thin brown dust that he had emptied out of his corridor.

Once he came at an early hour, as he often did, to wish her good-morning and ask if she had slept well.

"Not flying to-day?" he inquired.

"No, it's too windy."

It was windy. The wind rushed and roared and flung the branches into a mad tumult. The leaves looked ready to fly away. After each great gust the sky would brighten, and in the pale light the trees seemed balder. The pine in which Maya and Fridolin lived shrieked with the voices of the wind as in a fury of anger and excitement.

Fridolin sighed.

"I worked all night," he told Maya, "all night. But what can you do? You've got to do *some*thing to get *some*where. And I'm not altogether satisfied with this pine; I should have tackled a fir-tree." He wiped his brow and smiled in self-pity.

"How are your children?" asked Maya pleasantly.

"Thank you," said Fridolin, "thank you for your interest. But"--he hesitated--"but I don't supervise the way I used to. Still, I have reason to believe they are all doing well."

As he sat there, a little brown man with slightly curtailed wing-sheaths and a breastplate that looked like a head too large for its body, Maya thought he was almost comical; but she knew he was a dangerous beetle who could do immense harm to the mighty trees of the forest, and if his tribe attacked a tree in numbers then the green needles were doomed, the tree would turn sear and die. It

was utterly without defenses against the little
marauders who destroyed the bark and the sap-
wood. And the sap-wood is necessary to the life of a
tree because it carries the sap up to the very tips of
the branches. There were stories of how whole
forests had fallen victims to the race of boring-
beetles. Maya looked at Fridolin reflectively; she
was awed into solemnity at the thought of the great
power these little creatures possessed and of how
important they could become.

Fridolin sighed and said in a worried tone:

"Ah, life would be beautiful if there were no
woodpeckers."

Maya nodded.

"Yes, indeed, you're right. The woodpecker gobbles
up every insect he sees."

"If it were only that," observed Fridolin, "if it were
only that he got the careless people who fool around
on the outside, on the bark, I'd say, 'Very well, a
woodpecker must live too.' But it seems all wrong
that the bird should follow us right into our
corridors into the remotest corners of our homes."

"But he can't. He's too big, isn't he?"

Fridolin looked at Maya with an air of grave
importance, lifting his brows and shaking his head
two or three times. It seemed to please him that he
knew something she didn't know.

"Too big? What difference does his size make? No, my dear, it's not his size we are afraid of; it's his tongue."

Maya made big eyes.

Fridolin told her about the woodpecker's tongue: that it was long and thin, and round as a worm, and barbed and sticky.

"He can stretch his tongue out ten times my length," cried the bark-beetle, flourishing his arm. "You think: 'now--now he has reached the limit, he can't make it the tiniest bit longer.' But no, he goes on stretching and stretching it. He pokes it deep into all the cracks and crevices of the bark, on the chance that he'll find somebody sitting there. He even pushes it into our passageways--actually, into our corridors and chambers. Things stick to it, and that's the way he pulls us out of our homes."

"I am not a coward," said Maya, "I don't think I am, but what you say makes me creepy."

"Oh, *you're* all right," said Fridolin, a little envious, "you with your sting are safe. A person'll think twice before he'll let you sting his tongue. Anybody'll tell you that. But how about us bark-beetles? How do you think we feel? A cousin of mine got caught. We had just had a little quarrel on account of my wife. I remember every detail perfectly. My cousin was paying us a visit and hadn't yet got used to our ways or our arrangements. All of a sudden we heard a woodpecker scratching and boring--one of the smaller species. It must have

begun right at our building because as a rule we
hear him beforehand and have time to run to shelter
before he reaches us.

"Suddenly I heard my poor cousin scream in the
dark: 'Fridolin, I'm sticking!' Then all I heard was a
short desperate scuffle, followed by complete
silence, and in a few moments the woodpecker was
hammering at the house next door. My poor cousin!
Her name was Agatha."

"Feel how my heart is beating," said Maya, in a
whisper. "You oughtn't to have told it so quickly.
My goodness, the things that do happen!" And the
little bee thought of her own adventures in the past
and the accidents that might still happen to her.

A laugh from Fridolin interrupted her reflections.
She looked up in surprise.

"See who's coming," he cried, "coming up the tree.
Here's the fellow for you! I tell you, he's a--but
you'll see."

Maya followed the direction of his gaze and saw a
remarkable animal slowly climbing up the trunk.
She wouldn't have believed such a creature was
possible if she had not seen it with her own eyes.

"Hadn't we better hide?" she asked, alarm getting
the better of astonishment.

"Absurd," replied the bark-beetle, "just sit still and
be polite to the gentleman. He is very learned,
really, very scholarly, and what is more, kind and

modest and, like most persons of his type, rather funny. See what he's doing now!"

"Probably thinking," observed Maya, who couldn't get over her astonishment.

"He's struggling against the wind," said Fridolin, and laughed. "I hope his legs don't get entangled."

"Are those long threads really his legs?" asked Maya, opening her eyes wide. "I've never seen the like."

Meanwhile the newcomer had drawn near, and Maya got a better view of him. He looked as though he were swinging in the air, his rotund little body hung so high on his monstrously long legs, which groped for a footing on all sides like a movable scaffolding of threads. He stepped along cautiously, feeling his way; the little brown sphere of his body rose and sank, rose and sank. His legs were so very long and thin that one alone would certainly not have been enough to support his body. He needed all at once, unquestionably. As they were jointed in the middle, they rose high in the air above him.

Maya clapped her hands together.

"Well!" she cried. "Did you ever? Would you have dreamed that such delicate legs, legs as fine as a hair, could be so nimble and useful--that one could really use them--and they'd know what to do? Fridolin, I think it's wonderful, simply wonderful."

"Ah, bah," said the bark-beetle. "Don't take things

so seriously. Just laugh when you see something
funny; that's all."

"But I don't feel like laughing. Often we laugh at
something and later find out it was just because we
haven't understood."

By this time the stranger had joined them and was
looking down at Maya from the height of his
pointed triangles of legs.

"Good-morning," he said, "a real wind-storm--a
pretty strong draught, don't you think, or--no? You
are of a different opinion?" He clung to the tree as
hard as he could.

Fridolin turned to hide his laughing, but little Maya
replied politely that she quite agreed with him and
that was why she had not gone out flying. Then she
introduced herself. The stranger squinted down at
her through his legs.

"Maya, of the nation of bees," he repeated.
"Delighted, really. I have heard a good deal about
bees.-- I myself belong to the general family of
spiders, species daddy-long-legs, and my name is
Hannibal."

The word spider has an evil sound in the ears of all
smaller insects, and Maya could not quite conceal
her fright, especially as she was reminded of her
agony in Thekla's web. Hannibal seemed to take no
notice, so Maya decided, "Well if need be I'll fly
away, and he can whistle for me; he has no wings
and his web is somewhere else."

"I am thinking," said Hannibal, "thinking very hard.-- If you will permit me, I will come a little closer. That big branch there makes a good shield against the wind."

"Why, certainly," said Maya, making room for him.

Fridolin said good-by and left. Maya stayed; she was eager to get at Hannibal's personality.

"The many, many different kinds of animals there are in the world," she thought. "Every day a fresh discovery."

The wind had subsided some, and the sun shone through the branches. From below rose the song of a robin redbreast, filling the woods with joy. Maya could see it perched on a branch, could see its throat swell and pulse with the song as it held its little head raised up to the light.

"If only I could sing like that robin redbreast," she said, "I'd perch on a flower and keep it up the livelong day."

"You'd produce something lovely, you would, with your humming and buzzing."

"The bird looks so happy."

"You have great fancies," said the daddy-long-legs. "Supposing every animal were to wish he could do something that nature had not fitted him to do, the world would be all topsy-turvy. Supposing a robin redbreast thought he had to have a sting--a sting above everything else--or a goat wanted to fly about gathering honey. Supposing a frog were to come along and languish for my kind of legs."

Maya laughed.

"That isn't just what I mean. I mean, it seems lovely to be able to make all beings as happy as the bird does with his song.-- But goodness gracious!" she exclaimed suddenly. "Mr. Hannibal, you have one leg too many."

Hannibal frowned and looked into space, vexed.

"Well, you've noticed it," he said glumly. "But as a matter of fact--one leg too few, not too many."

"Why? Do you usually have eight legs?"

"Permit me to explain. We spiders have eight legs. We need them all. Besides, eight is a more aristocratic number. One of my legs got lost. Too bad about it. However you manage, you make the best of it."

"It must be dreadfully disagreeable to lose a leg," Maya sympathized.

Hannibal propped his chin on his hand and arranged his legs to keep them from being easily counted.

"I'll tell you how it happened. Of course, as usual when there's mischief, a human being is mixed up in it. We spiders are careful and look what we're doing, but human beings are careless, they grab you sometimes as though you were a piece of wood. Shall I tell you?"

"Oh, do please," said Maya, settling herself comfortably. "It would be awfully interesting. You must certainly have gone through a good deal."

"I should say so," said Hannibal. "Now listen. We daddy-long-legs, you know, hunt by night. I was then living in a green garden-house. It was overgrown with ivy, and there were a number of broken window-panes, which made it very convenient for me to crawl in and out. The man came at dark. In one hand he carried his artificial sun, which he calls lamp, in the other hand a small bottle, under his arm some paper, and in his pocket another bottle. He put everything down on the table and began to think, because he wanted to write his thoughts on the paper.-- You must certainly have come across paper in the woods or in the garden. The black on the paper is what man has excogitated--excogitated."

"Marvelous!" cried Maya, all a-glow that she was to learn so much.

"For this purpose," Hannibal continued, "man needs both bottles. He inserts a stick into the one and drinks out of the other. The more he drinks, the better it goes. Of course it is about us insects that he writes, everything he knows about us, and he writes strenuously, but the result is not much to boast of, because up to now man has found out very little in

regard to insects. He is absolutely ignorant of our
soul-life and hasn't the least consideration for our
feelings. You'll see."

"Don't you think well of human beings?" asked
Maya.

"Oh, yes, yes. But the loss of a leg"--the daddy-
long-legs looked down slantwise--"is apt to
embitter one, rather."

"I see," said Maya.

"One evening I was sitting on a window-frame as
usual, prepared for the chase, and the man was
sitting at the table, his two bottles before him,
trying to produce something. It annoyed me
dreadfully that a whole swarm of little flies and
gnats, upon which I depend for my subsistence, had
settled upon the artificial sun and were staring into
it in that crude, stupid, uneducated way of theirs."

"Well," observed Maya, "I think I'd look at a thing
like that myself."

"Look, for all I care. But to look and to stare like an
idiot are two entirely different things. Just watch
once and see the silly jig they dance around a lamp.
It's nothing for them to butt their heads about
twenty times. Some of them keep it up until they
burn their wings. And all the time they stare and
stare at the light."

"Poor creatures! Evidently they lose their wits."

"Then they had better stay outside on the window-frame or under the leaves. They're safe from the lamp there, and that's where I can catch them.-- Well, on that fateful night I saw from my position on the window-frame that some gnats were lying scattered on the table beside the lamp drawing their last breath. The man did not seem to notice or care about them, so I decided to go and take them myself. That's perfectly natural, isn't it?"

"Perfectly."

"And yet, it was my undoing. I crept up the leg of the table, very softly, on my guard, until I could peep over the edge. The man seemed dreadfully big. I watched him working. Then, slowly, very slowly, carefully lifting one leg at a time, I crossed over to the lamp. As long as I was covered by the bottle all went well, but I had scarcely turned the corner, when the man looked up and grabbed me. He lifted me by one of my legs, dangled me in front of his huge eyes, and said: 'See what's here, just see what's here.' And he grinned--the brute!--he grinned with his whole face, as though it were a laughing matter."

Hannibal sighed, and little Maya kept quite still. Her head was in a whirl.

"Have human beings such immense eyes?" she asked at last.

"Please think of *me* in the position *I* was in," cried Hannibal, vexed. "Try to imagine how I felt. Who'd like to be hanging by the leg in front of eyes twenty

times as big as his own body and a mouth full of
gleaming teeth, each fully twice as big as himself?
Well, what do you think?"

"Awful! Perfectly awful!"

"Thank the Lord, my leg broke off. There's no
telling what might have happened if my leg had not
broken off. I fell to the table, and then I ran, I ran as
fast as my remaining legs would take me, and hid
behind the bottle. There I stood and hurled threats
of violence at the man. They saved me, my threats
did, the man was afraid to run after me. I saw him
lay my leg on the white paper, and I watched how it
wanted to escape--which it can't do without me."

"Was it still moving?" asked Maya, prickling at the
thought.

"Yes. Our legs always do move when they're pulled
out. My leg ran, but I not being there it didn't know
where to run to, so it merely flopped about
aimlessly on the same spot, and the man watched it,
clutching at his nose and smiling--smiling, the
heartless wretch!--at my leg's sense of duty."

"Impossible," said the little bee, quite scared, "an
offen leg can't crawl."

"An offen leg? *What* is an offen leg?"

"A leg that has come off," explained Maya, staring
at him. "Don't you know? At home we children
used the word offen for anything that had come
off."

"You should drop your nursery slang when you're out in the world and in the presence of cultured people," said Hannibal severely. "But it *is* true that our legs totter long after they have been torn from our bodies."

"I can't believe it without proof."

"Do you think I'll tear one of my legs off to satisfy you?" Hannibal's tone was ugly. "I see you're not a fit person to associate with. Nobody, I'd like you to know, *no*body has ever doubted my word before."

Maya was terribly put out. She couldn't understand what had upset the daddy-long-legs so, or what dreadful thing she had done.

"It isn't altogether easy to get along with strangers," she thought. "They don't think the way we do and don't see that we mean no harm." She was depressed and cast a troubled look at the spider with his long legs and soured expression.

"Really, someone ought to come and eat you up."

Hannibal had evidently mistaken Maya's good nature for weakness. For now something unusual happened to the little bee. Suddenly her depression passed and gave way, not to alarm or timidity, but to a calm courage. She straightened up, lifted her lovely, transparent wings, uttered her high clear buzz, and said with a gleam in her eyes:

"I am a bee, Mr. Hannibal."

"I beg your pardon," said he, and without saying good-by turned and ran down the tree-trunk as fast as a person can run who has seven legs.

Maya had to laugh, willy-nilly. From down below Hannibal began to scold.

"You're bad. You threaten helpless people, you threaten them with your sting when you know they're handicapped by a misfortune and can't get away fast. But your hour is coming, and when you're in a tight place you'll think of me and be sorry." Hannibal disappeared under the leaves of the coltsfoot on the ground. His last words had not reached the little bee.

The wind had almost died away, and the day promised to be fine. White clouds sailed aloft in a deep, deep blue, looking happy and serene like good thoughts of the Lord. Maya was cheered. She thought of the rich shaded meadows by the woods and of the sunny slopes beyond the lake. A blithe activity must have begun there by this time. In her mind she saw the slim grasses waving and the purple iris that grew in the rills at the edge of the woods. From the flower of an iris you could look across to the mysterious night of the pine-forest and catch its cool breath of melancholy. You knew that its forbidding silence, which transformed the sunshine into a reddish half-light of sleep, was the home of the fairy tale.

Maya was already flying. She had started off instinctively, in answer to the call of the meadows and their gay carpeting of flowers. It was a joy to be alive.

CHAPTER X

THE WONDERS OF THE NIGHT

Thus the days and weeks of her young life passed for little Maya among the insects in a lovely summer world--a happy roving in garden and meadow, occasional risks and many joys. For all that, she often missed the companions of her early childhood and now and again suffered a pang of homesickness, an ache of longing for her people and the kingdom she had left. There were hours, too, when she yearned for regular, useful work and association with friends of her own kind.

However, at bottom she had a restless nature, little Maya had, and was scarcely ready to settle down for good and live in the community of the bees; she wouldn't have felt comfortable. Often among animals as well as human beings there are some who cannot conform to the ways of the others. Before we condemn them we must be careful and give them a chance to prove themselves. For it is not always laziness or stubbornness that makes them different. Far from it. At the back of their peculiar urge is a deep longing for something higher or better than what every-day life has to offer, and many a time young runaways have grown up into good, sensible, experienced men and women.

Little Maya was a pure, sensitive soul, and her

attitude to the big, beautiful world came of a genuine eagerness for knowledge and a great delight in the glories of creation.

Yet it is hard to be alone even when you are happy, and the more Maya went through, the greater became her yearning for companionship and love. She was no longer so very young; she had grown into a strong, superb creature with sound, bright wings, a sharp, dangerous sting, and a highly developed sense of both the pleasures and the hazards of her life. Through her own experience she had gathered information and stored up wisdom, which she now often wished she could apply to something of real value. There were days when she was ready to return to the hive and throw herself at the queen's feet and sue for pardon and honorable reinstatement. But a great, burning desire held her back--the desire to know human beings. She had heard so many contradictory things about them that she was confused rather than enlightened. Yet she had a feeling that in the whole of creation there were no beings more powerful or more intelligent or more sublime than they.

A few times in her wanderings she had seen people, but only from afar, from high up in the air--big and little people, black people, white people, red people, and such as dressed in many colors. She had never ventured close. Once she had caught the glimmer of red near a brook, and thinking it was a bed of flowers had flown down. She found a human being fast asleep among the brookside blossoms. It had golden hair and a pink face and wore a red dress. It was dreadfully large, of course, but still it looked so good and sweet that Maya thrilled, and tears came to her eyes. She lost all sense of her whereabouts; she could do nothing but gaze and gaze upon the slumbering presence. All the horrid things she had ever heard against man seemed utterly impossible. Lies they must have been--mean lies that she had been told against creatures as charming as this one asleep in the shade of the whispering birch-trees.

After a while a mosquito came and buzzed greetings.

"Look!" cried Maya, hot with excitement and delight. "Look, just look at that human being there. How good, how beautiful! Doesn't it fill you with enthusiasm?"

The mosquito gave Maya a surprised stare, then turned slowly round to glance at the object of her admiration.

"Yes, it *is* good. I just tasted it. I stung it. Look, my body is shining red with its blood."

Maya had to press her hand to her heart, so startled was she by the mosquito's daring.

"Will it die?" she cried. "Where did you wound it? How could you? How could you screw up your courage to sting it? And how vile! Why, you're a beast of prey!"

The mosquito tittered.

"Why, it's only a very little human being," it answered in its high, thin voice. "It's the size called girl--the size at which the legs are covered half way up with a separate colored casing. My sting, of course, goes through the casing but usually doesn't reach the skin.-- Your ignorance is really stupendous. Do you actually think that human beings are good? I haven't come across one who willingly let me take the tiniest drop of his blood."

"I don't know very much about human beings, I admit," said Maya humbly.

"But of all the insects you bees have most to do with human beings. That's a well-known fact."

"I left our kingdom," Maya confessed timidly. "I didn't like it. I wanted to learn about the outside world."

"Well, well, what do you think of that!" The mosquito drew a step nearer. "How do you like your free-lancing? I must say, I admire you for your independence. I for one would never consent to serve human beings."

"But they serve us too!" said Maya, who couldn't bear a slight to be put upon her people.

"Maybe.-- To what nation do you belong?"

"I come of the nation in the castle park. The ruling queen is Helen VIII."

"Indeed," said the mosquito, and bowed low. "An enviable lineage. My deepest respects.-- There was a revolution in your kingdom not so long ago, wasn't there? I heard it from the messengers of the rebel swarm. Am I right?"

"Yes," said Maya, proud and happy that her nation was so respected and renowned. Homesickness for her people awoke again, deep down in her heart, and she wished she could do something good and great for her queen and country. Carried away on the wings of this dream, she forgot to ask about human beings. Or, like as not, she refrained from questions, feeling that the mosquito would not tell her things she would be glad to hear. The mite of a creature impressed her as a saucy Miss, and people of her kind usually had nothing good to say of others. Besides, she soon flew away.

"I'm going to take one more drink," she called back to Maya. "Later I and my friends are going flying in the light of the westering sun. Then we'll be sure to have good weather to-morrow."

Maya made off quickly. She couldn't bear to stay and see the mosquito hurt the sleeping child. And how could she do this thing and not perish? Hadn't Cassandra said: "If you sting a human being, you will die?"

Maya still remembered every detail of this incident with the child and the mosquito, but her craving to know human beings well had not been stilled. She made up her mind to be bolder and never stop trying until she had reached her goal.

At last Maya's longing to know human beings was to be satisfied, and in a way far, far lovelier and more wonderful than she had dreamed.

Once, on a warm evening, having gone to sleep earlier than usual, she woke up suddenly in the middle of the night--something that had never happened to her before. When she opened her eyes, her astonishment was indescribable: her little bedroom was all steeped in a quiet bluish radiance. It came down through the entrance, and the entrance itself shone as if hung with a silver-blue curtain.

Maya did not dare to budge at first, though not because she was frightened. No. Somehow, along with the light came a rare, lovely peacefulness, and outside her room the air was filled with a sound finer, more harmonious than any music she had ever heard. After a time she rose timidly, awed by the glamour and the strangeness of it all, and looked out. The whole world seemed to lie under the spell of an enchantment. Everything was sparkling and glittering in pure silver. The trunks of the birch-trees, the slumbering leaves were overlaid with silver. The grass, which from her height seemed to lie under delicate veils, was set with a thousand pale pearls. All things near and far, the silent distances, were shrouded in this soft, bluish sheen.

"This must be the night," Maya whispered and folded her hands.

High up in the heavens, partly veiled by the leaves of a beech-tree, hung a full clear disk of silver, from which the radiance poured down that beautified the world. And then Maya saw countless bright, sharp little lights surrounding the moon in the heavens-- oh, so still and beautiful, unlike any shining things she had ever seen before. To think she beheld the night, the moon, and the stars--the wonders, the lovely wonders of the night! She had heard of them but never believed in them. It was almost too much.

Then the sound rose again, the strange night sound that must have awakened her. It came from nearby, filling the welkin, a soaring chirp with a silvery ring that matched the silver on the trees and leaves and grass and seemed to come rilling down from the moon on the beams of silver light.

Maya looked about for the source, in vain; in the mysterious drift of light and shadow it was difficult to make out objects in clear outline, everything was draped so mysteriously; and yet everything showed up true and in such heroic beauty.

Her room could keep her no longer; out she had to fly into this new splendor, the night splendor.

"The good Lord will take care of me," she thought, "I am not bent upon wrong."

As she was about to fly off through the silver light to her favorite meadow, now lying full under the moon, she saw a winged creature alight on a beech-tree leaf not far away. Scarcely alighted, it raised its head to the moon, lifted its narrow wings, and drew the edge of one against the other, for all the world as though it were playing on a violin. And sure enough, the sound came, the silvery chirp that filled the whole moonlit world with melody.

"Exquisite," whispered Maya, "heavenly, heavenly, heavenly."

She flew over to the leaf. The night was so mild and warm that she did not notice it was cooler than by day. When she touched the leaf, the chirper broke off playing abruptly, and to Maya it seemed as if there had never been such a stillness before, so profound was the hush that followed. It was uncanny. Through the dark leaves filtered the light, white and cool.

"Good night," said Maya, politely, thinking "good night" was the greeting for the night like "good morning" for the morning. "Please excuse me for interrupting, but the music you make is so fascinating that I had to find out where it came from."

The chirper stared at Maya, wide-eyed.

"What sort of a crawling creature are you?" it asked after some moments had passed. "I have never met one like you before."

"I am not a crawling insect. I am Maya, of the nation of bees."

"Oh, of the nation of bees. Indeed ... you live by day, don't you? I have heard of your race from the hedgehog. He told me that in the evening he eats the dead bodies that are thrown out of your hive."

"Yes," said Maya, with a faint chill of apprehension, "that's so; Cassandra told me about him; she heard of him from the sentinels. He comes when twilight falls and snouts in the grass looking for dead bodies.-- But do you associate with the hedgehog? Why, he's an awful brute."

"I don't think so. We tree-crickets get along with him splendidly. We call him Uncle. Of course he always tries to catch us, but he never succeeds, so we have great fun teasing him. Everybody has to live, doesn't he? Just so he doesn't live off me, what do I care?"

Maya shook her head. She didn't agree. But not caring to insult the cricket by contradicting, she changed the subject.

"So you're a tree-cricket?"

"Yes, a snowy tree-cricket.-- But I must play, so please don't keep me any longer. It's full moon, a wonderful night. I must play."

"Oh, do make an exception this once. You play all the time.-- Tell me about the night."

"A midsummer night is the loveliest in the world," answered the cricket. "It fills the heart with rapture.-- But what my music doesn't tell you I shan't be able to explain. Why *need* everything be explained? Why *know* everything? We poor creatures can find out only the tiniest bit about existence. Yet we can *feel* the glory of the whole wide world." And the cricket set up its happy

silvery strumming. Heard from close by, where
Maya sat, the music was overpowering in its
loudness.

The little bee sat quite still in the blue summer night
listening and musing deeply about life and creation.

Silence fell. There was a faint whirr, and Maya saw
the cricket fly out into the moonlight.

"The night makes one feel sad," she reflected.

Her flowery meadow drew her now. She flew off.

At the edge of the brook stood the tall irises
brokenly reflected in the running water. A glorious
sight. The moonlight was whirled along in the
braided current, the wavelets winked and
whispered, the irises seemed to lean over asleep.
"Asleep from sheer delight," thought the little bee.
She dropped down on a blue petal in the full light of
the moon and could not take her eyes from the
living waters of the brook, the quivering flash, the
flashing come and go of countless sparks. On the
bank opposite, the birch-trees glittered as if hung
with the stars.

"Where is all that water flowing to?" she wondered.
"The cricket is right. We know so little about the
world."

Of a sudden a fine little voice rose in song from the
flower of an iris close beside her, ringing like a
pure, clear bell, different from any earthly sound
that Maya knew. Her heart throbbed, she held her

breath.

"Oh, what is going to happen? What am I going to see now?"

The iris swayed gently. One of the petals curved in at the edge, and Maya saw a tiny snow-white human hand holding on to the flower's rim with its wee little fingers. Then a small blond head arose, and then a delicate luminous body in white garments. A human being in miniature was coming up out of the iris.

Words cannot tell Maya's awe and rapture. She sat rigid.

The tiny being climbed to the edge of the blossom, lifted its arms up to the moonlight, and looked out into the bright shining night with a smile of bliss lighting up its face. Then a faint quiver shook its luminous body, and from its shoulders two wings unfolded, whiter than the moonlight, pure as snow, rising above its blond head and reaching down to its feet. How lovely it was, how exquisitely lovely. Nothing that Maya had ever seen compared with it in loveliness.

Standing there in the moonlight, holding its hands up to heaven, the luminous little being lifted its voice again and sang. The song rang out in the night, and Maya understood the words.

My home is Light. The crystal bowl Of Heaven's blue, I love it so! Both Death and Life will change, I know, But not my soul, my living soul.

My soul is that which breathes anew From all of loveliness and grace; And as it flows from God's own face, It flows from His creations, too.

Maya burst into sobs. What it was that made her so sad and yet so happy, she could not have told.

The little human being turned around.

"Who is crying?" he asked in his chiming voice.

"It's only me," stammered Maya. "Excuse me for interrupting you."

"But why are you crying?"

"I don't know. Perhaps just because you are so beautiful. Who are you? Oh, do tell me, if I am not asking too much. You are an angel, aren't you? You must be."

"Oh, no," said the little creature, quite serious. "I am only a sprite, a flower-sprite.-- But, dear little bee, what are you doing out here in the meadow so late at night?"

The sprite flew over to a curving iris blade beside Maya and regarded her long and kindly from his swaying perch in the moonlight.

Maya told him all about herself, what she had done, what she knew, and what she longed for. And while she spoke, his eyes never left her, those large dark eyes glowing in the white fairy face under the golden hair that ever and anon shone like silver in the moonlight.

When she finished he stroked her head and looked at her so warmly and lovingly that the little bee, beside herself with joy, had to lower her gaze.

"We sprites," he explained, "live seven nights, but we must stay in the flower in which we are born, else we die at dawn."

Maya opened her eyes wide in terror.

"Then hurry, hurry! Fly back into your flower!"

The, sprite shook his head sadly.

"Too late.-- But listen. I have more to tell you. Most of us sprites are glad to leave our flowers never to return, because a great happiness is connected with our leaving. We are endowed with a remarkable power: before we die, we can fulfill the dearest wish of the first creature we meet. It is when we make up our minds seriously to leave the flower for the purpose of making someone happy that our wings grow."

"How wonderful!" cried Maya. "I'd leave the flower too, then. It must be lovely to fulfill another person's wish." That *she* was the first being whom the sprite on his flight from the flower had met, did not occur to her. "And then--must you die?"

The sprite nodded, but not sadly this time.

"We live to see the dawn still," he said, "but when the dew falls, we are drawn into the fine cobwebby veils that float above the grass and the flowers of the meadows. Haven't you often noticed that the veils shine white as though a light were inside them? It's the sprites, their wings and their garments. When the light rises we change into dew-drops. The plants drink us and we become a part of their growing and blooming until in time we rise again as sprites from out their flowers."

"Then you were once another sprite?" asked Maya, tense, breathless with interest.

The earnest eyes said yes.

"But I have forgotten my earlier existence. We forget everything in our flower-sleep."

"Oh, what a lovely fate!"

"It is the same as that of all earthly creatures, when you really come to think of it, even if it isn't always flowers out of which they wake up from their sleep of death. But we won't talk of that to-night."

"Oh, I'm so happy!" cried Maya.

"Then you haven't got a wish? You're the first person I've met, you know, and I possess the power to grant your dearest wish."

"I? But I'm only a bee. No, it's too much. It would be too great a joy. I don't deserve it, I don't deserve that you should be so good to me."

"No one deserves the good and the beautiful. The good and the beautiful come to us like the sunshine."

Maya's heart beat stormily. Oh, she did have a wish, a burning wish, but she didn't dare confess it. The elf seemed to guess; he smiled so you couldn't keep anything a secret from him.

"Well?" He stroked his golden hair off his pure forehead.

"I'd like to know human beings at their best and most beautiful," said the little bee. She spoke quickly and hotly. She was afraid she would be told that so great a wish could not be granted.

But the sprite drew himself up, his expression was serious and serene, his eyes shone with confidence. He took Maya's trembling hand and said:

"Come. We'll fly together. Your wish shall be granted."

CHAPTER XI

WITH THE SPRITE

And so Maya and the flower-sprite started off together in the bright mid-summer night, flying low over the blossomy meadow. His white reflection crossing the brook shone as though a star were gliding through the water.

How happy the little bee was to confide herself to this gracious being! Whatever he were to do, wherever he were to lead her would be good and right, she felt. She would have liked to ask him a thousand questions had she dared.

As they were passing between a double row of high poplar-trees, something whirred above them; a dark moth, as big and strong as a bird, crossed their way.

"One moment, wait one moment, please," the sprite called.

Maya was surprised to see how readily the moth responded.

All three alighted on a high poplar branch, from which there was a far view out upon the tranquil, moonlit landscape. The quaking leaves whispered delicately. The moth, perching directly opposite Maya in the full light of the moon, slowly lifted his spread wings and dropped them again, softly, as if gently fanning--fanning a cool breath upon someone. Broad, diagonal stripes of a gorgeous bright blue marked his wings, his black head was covered as with dark velvet, his face was like a strangely mysterious mask, out of which glowed a pair of dark eyes. How wonderful were the creatures of the night! A little cold shiver ran through Maya, who felt she was dreaming the strangest dream of her life.

"You are beautiful," she said to the moth,
"beautiful, really." She was awed and solemn.

"Who is your companion?" the moth asked the
sprite.

"A bee. I met her just as I was leaving my flower."

The moth seemed to realize what that meant. He
looked at Maya almost enviously.

"You fortunate creature!" he said in a low, serious,
musing tone, shaking his head to and fro.

"Are you sad?" asked Maya out of the warmth of
her heart.

The moth shook his head.

"No, not sad." His voice sounded friendly and
grateful, and he gave Maya such a kind look that
she would have liked to strike up a friendship with
him then and there.

"Is the bat still abroad, or has he gone to rest?" This
was the question for which the sprite had stopped
the moth.

"Oh, he's gone to rest long ago. You want to know,
do you, on account of your companion?"

The sprite nodded. Maya was dying to find out what
a bat was, but the sprite seemed to be in a hurry.
With a charming gesture of restlessness he tossed

his shining hair back from his forehead.

"Come, Maya," he said, "we must hurry. The night is so short."

"Shall I carry you part of the way?" asked the moth.

The sprite thanked him but declined. "Some other time!" he called.

"Then it will be never," thought Maya as they flew away, "because at dawn the flower-sprite must die."

The moth remained on the leaf looking after them until the glimmer of the fairy garments grew smaller and smaller and finally sank into the depths of the blue distance. Then he turned his face slowly and surveyed his great dark wings with their broad blue stripes. He sank into revery.

"So often I have heard that I am gray and ugly," he said to himself, "and that my dress is not to be compared with the superb robes of the butterfly. But the little bee saw only what is beautiful in me.-- And she asked me if I was sad. I wonder whether I am or not.-- No, I am not sad," he decided, "not now."

Meanwhile Maya and the flower-sprite flew through the dense shrubbery of a garden. The glory of it in the dimmed moonlight was beyond the power of mortal lips to say. An intoxicatingly sweet cool breath of dew and slumbering flowers transformed all things into unutterable blessings. The lilac grapes of the acacias sparkled in freshness, the June rose-tree looked like a small blooming heaven hung with red lamps, the white stars of the jasmine glowed palely, sadly, and poured out their perfume as if, in this one hour, to make a gift of their all.

Maya was dazed. She pressed the sprite's hand and looked at him. A light of bliss shone from his eyes.

"Who could have dreamed of this!" whispered the little bee.

Just then she saw something that sent a pang through her.

"Oh," she cried, "look! A star has fallen! It's straying about and can't find its way back to its place in the sky."

"That's a firefly," said the flower-sprite, without a smile.

Now, in the midst of her amazement, Maya realized for the first time why the sprite seemed so dear and kind. He never laughed at her ignorance; on the contrary, he helped her when she went wrong.

"They are odd little creatures," the sprite continued. "They carry their own light about with them on warm summer nights and enliven the dark under the shrubbery where the moonlight doesn't shine through. So firefly can keep tryst with firefly even in the dark. Later, when we come to the human beings, you will make the acquaintance of one of them."

"Why?" asked Maya.

"You'll soon see."

By this time they had reached an arbor completely overgrown with jasmine and woodbine. They descended almost to the ground. From close by, within the arbor, came the sound of faint whispering. The flower-sprite beckoned to a firefly.

"Would you be good enough," he asked, "to give us a little light? We have to push through these dark leaves here; we want to get to the inside of the jasmine-arbor."

"But your glow is much brighter than mine."

"I think so, too," put in Maya, more to hide her excitement than anything else.

"I must wrap myself up in a leaf," explained the sprite, "else the human beings would see me and be frightened. We sprites appear to human beings only in their dreams."

"I see," said the firefly. "I am at your service. I will do what I can.-- Won't the great beast with you hurt me?"

The sprite shook his head no, and the firefly believed him.

The sprite now took a leaf and wrapped himself in it; the gleam of his white garments was completely hidden. Then he picked a little bluebell from the grass and put it on his shining head like a helmet. The only bit of him left exposed was his face, which was so small that surely no one would notice it. He asked the firefly to perch on his shoulder and with its wing to dim its lamp on the one side so as to keep the dazzle out of his eyes.

"Come now," he said, taking Maya's hand. "We had better climb up right here."

The little bee was thinking of something the sprite had said, and as they clambered up the vine, she asked:

"Do human beings dream when they sleep?"

"Not only then. They dream sometimes even when they are awake. They sit with their bodies a little limp, their heads bent a little forward, and their eyes searching the distance, as if to see into the very heavens. Their dreams are always lovelier than life. That's why we appear to them in their dreams."

The sprite now laid his tiny finger on his lips, bent aside a small blooming sprig of jasmine, and gently pushed Maya ahead.

"Look down," he said softly, "you'll see what you have been wishing to see."

The little bee looked and saw two human beings sitting on a bench in the shadows cast by the moonlight--a boy and a girl, the girl with her head leaning on the boy's shoulder, and the boy holding his arm around the girl as if to protect her. They sat in complete stillness, looking wide-eyed into the night. It was as quiet as if they had both gone to sleep. Only from a distance came the chirping of the crickets, and slowly, slowly the moonlight drifted through the leaves.

Maya, transported out of herself, gazed into the girl's face. Although it looked pale and wistful, it seemed to be transfused by the hidden radiance of a great happiness. Above her large eyes lay golden hair, like the golden hair of the sprite, and upon it rested the heavenly sheen of the midsummer night. From her red lips, slightly parted, came a breath of rapture and melancholy, as if she wanted to offer everything that was hers to the man by her side for his happiness.

And now she turned to him, pulled his head down, and whispered a magical something that brought a smile to his face such as Maya thought no earthly being could wear. In his eyes gleamed a happiness and a vigor as if the whole big world were his to own, and suffering and misfortune were banished forever from the face of the earth.

Maya somehow had no desire to know what he said to the girl in reply. Her heart quivered as though the ecstasy that emanated from the two human beings was also hers.

"Now I have seen the most glorious thing that my eyes will ever behold," she whispered to herself. "I know now that human beings are most beautiful when they are in love."

How long Maya stayed behind the leaves without stirring, lost in looking at the boy and girl, she did not know. When she turned round, the firefly's lamp had been extinguished, the sprite was gone.
Through the doorway of the arbor far across the country on the distant horizon showed a narrow streak of red.

CHAPTER XII

ALOIS, LADYBIRD AND POET

The sun was risen high above the tops of the beech-trees when Maya awoke in her woodland retreat. In the first moments, the moonlight, the chirping of the cricket, the midsummer night meadow, the lovely sprite, the boy and the girl in the arbor, all seemed the perishing fancies of a delicious dream. Yet here it was almost midday; and she remembered slipping back into her chamber in the chill of dawn. So it had all been real, she *had* spent the night with the flower-sprite and *had* seen the two human beings, with their arms round each other, in the arbor of woodbine and jasmine.

The sun outside was glowing hot on the leaves, a warm wind was stirring, and Maya heard the mixed chorus of thousands of insects. Ah, what these knew, and what *she* knew! So proud was she of the great thing that had happened to her that she couldn't get out to the others fast enough; she thought they must read it in her very looks.

But in the sunlight everything was the same as ever.
Nothing was changed; nothing recalled the blue
moonlit night. The insects came, said how-do-you-
do, and left; yonder, the meadow was a scene of
bustling activity; the insects, birds and butterflies
hopped, flew and flitted in the hot flickering air
around the tall, gay midsummer flowers.

Sadness fell upon Maya. There was no one in the
world to share her joys and sorrows. She couldn't
make up her mind to fly over and join the others in
the meadow. No, she would go to the woods. The
woods were serious and solemn. They suited her
mood.

How many mysteries and marvels lie hidden in the
dim depths of the woods, no one suspects who
hurries unobservant along the beaten tracks. You
must bend aside the branches of the underbrush, or
lean down and peep between the blackberry briars
through the tall grasses and across the thick moss.
Under the shaded leaves of the plants, in holes in
the ground and tree-trunks, in the decaying bark of
stumps, in the curl and twist of the roots that coil on
the ground like serpents, there is an active,
multiform life by day and by night, full of joys and
dangers, struggles and sorrows and pleasures.

Maya divined only a little of this as she flew low
between the dark-brown trunks under the leafy roof
of green. She followed a narrow trail in the grass,
which made a clear path through thicket and
clearing. Now and then the sun seemed to disappear
behind clouds, so deep was the shade under the high
foliage and in the close shrubbery; but soon she was

flying again through a bright shimmer of gold and green above the broad-leaved miniature forests of bracken and blackberry.

After a long stretch the woods opened their columned and over-arched portals; before Maya's eyes lay a wide field of grain in the golden sunshine. Butterfly-weed flamed on the grassy borders. She alighted on the branch of a birch-tree at the edge of the field and gazed upon the sea of gold that spread out endlessly in the tranquillity of the placid day. It rippled softly under the shy summer breeze, which blew gently so as not to disturb the peace of the lovely world.

Under the birch-tree a few small brown butterflies, using the butterfly-weed for corners, were playing puss-in-the-corner, a favorite game with butterfly-children. Maya watched them a while.

"It must be lots of fun," she thought, "and the children in the hive might be taught to play it, too. The cells would do for corners.-- But Cassandra, I suppose, wouldn't permit it. She's so strict."

Ah, now Maya felt sad again. Because she had thought of home. And she was about to drift off into homesick revery when she heard someone beside her say:

"Good morning. You're a beast, it seems to me."

Maya turned with a start.

"No," she said, "decidedly not."

There sitting on her leaf was a little polished terra-
cotta half-sphere with seven black dots on its cupola
of a back, a minute black head and bright little eyes.
Peeping from under the dotted dome and supporting
it as best they could Maya detected thin legs fine as
threads. In spite of his queer figure, she somehow
took a great liking to the stout little fellow; he had
distinct charm.

"May I ask who you are? I myself am Maya of the
nation of bees."

"Do you mean to insult me? You have no reason
to."

"But why should I? I don't know you, really I
don't." Maya was quite upset.

"It's easy to *say* you don't know me.-- Well, I'll jog
your memory. Count." And the little rotundity
began to wheel round slowly.

"You mean I'm to count your dots?"

"Yes, if you please."

"Seven," said Maya.

"Well?-- Well? You still don't know. All right then,
I'll tell you. I'm called exactly according to what
you counted. The scientific name of our family is
Septempunctata. *Septem* is Latin for seven,
punctata is Latin for dots, points, you see. Our
common name is ladybird, my own name is Alois, I

am a poet by profession. You know our common name, of course."

Maya, afraid of hurting Alois' feelings, didn't dare to say no.

"Oh," said he, "I live by the sunshine, by the peace of the day, and by the love of mankind."

"But don't you eat, too?" asked Maya, quite astonished.

"Of course. Plant-lice. Don't you?"

"No. That would be--that is...."

"Is what? Is what?"

"Not--usual," said Maya shyly.

"Of course, of course!" cried Alois, trying to raise one shoulder, but not succeeding, on account of the firm set of his dome. "As a bourgeoise you would, of course, do only what is usual. We poets would not get very far that way.-- Have you time?"

"Why, yes," said Maya.

"Then I'll recite you one of my poems. Sit real still and close your eyes, so that nothing distracts your attention. The poem is called *Man's Finger*, and is about a personal experience. Are you listening?"

"Yes, to every word."

"Well, then:

"'Since you did not do me wrong, That you found me, doesn't matter. You are rounded, you are long; Up above you wear a flatter, Pointed, polished sheath or platter Which you move as swift as light, But below you're fastened tight!'"

"Well?" asked Alois after a short pause. There were tears in his eyes and a quaver in his voice.

"*Man's Finger* gripped me very hard," replied Maya in some embarrassment. She really knew much lovelier poems.

"How do you find the form?" Alois questioned with a smile of fine melancholy. He seemed to be overwhelmed by the effect he had produced.

"Long and round. You yourself said so in the poem."

"I mean the artistic form, the form of my verse."

"Oh--oh, yes. Yes, I thought it was very good."

"It is, isn't it!" cried Alois. "What you mean to say is that *Man's Finger* may be ranked among the best poems you know of, and one must go way back in literature before one comes across anything like it. The prime requisite in art is that it should contain something new, which is what most poets forget. And bigness, too. Don't you agree with me?"

"Certainly," said Maya, "I think...."

"The firm belief you express in my importance as a poet really overwhelms me. I thank you.-- But I must be going now, for solitude is the poet's pride. Farewell."

"Farewell," echoed Maya, who really didn't know just what the little fellow had been after.

"Well," she thought, "*he* knows. Perhaps he's not full grown yet; he certainly isn't large." She looked after him, as he hastened up the branch. His wee legs were scarcely visible; he looked as though he were moving on low rollers.

Maya turned her gaze away, back to the golden field of grain over which the butterflies were playing. The field and the butterflies gave her ever so much more pleasure than the poetry of Alois, ladybird and poet.

CHAPTER XIII

THE FORTRESS

How happily the day had begun and how miserably it was to end!

Before the horror swept upon her, Maya had formed a very remarkable acquaintance. It was in the afternoon near a big old water-butt. She was sitting amid the scented elder blossoms, which lay mirrored in the placid dark surface of the butt, and a robin redbreast was warbling overhead, so sweetly and merrily that Maya thought it was a shame, a crying shame that she, a bee, could not make friends with the charming songsters. The trouble was, they were too big and ate you up.

She had hidden herself in the heart of the elder blossoms and was listening and blinking under the pointed darts of the sunlight, when she heard someone beside her sigh. Turning round she saw-- well, now it really *was* the strangest of all the strange creatures she had ever met. It must have had at least a hundred legs along each side of its body-- so she thought at first glance. It was about three times her size, and slim, low, and wingless.

"For goodness sake! Mercy on me!" Maya was quite startled. "You must certainly be able to run!"

The stranger gave her a pondering look.

"I doubt it," he said. "I doubt it. There's room for improvement. I have too many legs. You see, before all my legs can be set in motion, too much time is lost. I didn't use to realize this, and often wished I had a few more legs. But God's will be done.-- Who are you?"

Maya introduced herself. The other one nodded and moved some of his legs.

"I am Thomas of the family of millepeds. We are an old race, and we arouse admiration and astonishment in all parts of the globe. No other animals can boast anything like our number of legs. Eight is *their* limit, so far as I know."

"You are tremendously interesting. And your color is so queer. Have you got a family?"

"Why, no! Why should I? What good would a family do me? We millepeds crawl out of our eggs; that's all. If *we* can't stand on our own feet, who should?"

"Of course, of course," Maya observed thoughtfully. "But have you no relations?"

"No, dear child. I earn my living, and doubt. I doubt."

"Oh! *What* do you doubt?"

"I was born doubting. I must doubt."

Maya stared at him in wide-eyed bewilderment. What did he mean, what could he possibly mean? She couldn't for the life of her make out, but she did not want to pry too curiously into his private affairs.

"For one thing," said Thomas after a pause, "for one thing I doubt whether you have chosen a good place to rest in. Don't you know what's over there in the big willow?"

"No."

"You see! I doubted right away if you knew. The

city of the hornets is over there."

Maya turned deathly white and nearly fell off the elder blossoms. In a voice shaking with fright, she asked just where the city was.

"Do you see that old nesting-box for starlings, there in the shrubbery near the trunk of the willow-tree? It's so poorly placed that I doubted from the first whether starlings would ever move in. If a bird-house isn't set with its door facing the sunrise, every decent bird will think twice before taking possession. Well, the hornets have entrenched themselves in it. It's the biggest hornets' fortress in the country. You as a bee certainly ought to know of the place. Why, the hornets are brigands who lie in wait for you bees. So, at least, I have observed."

Maya scarcely heard what he was saying. There, showing clear against the green, she saw the brown walls of the fortress. She almost stopped breathing.

"I must fly away," she cried.

Too late! Behind her sounded a loud, mean laugh. At the same moment the little bee felt herself caught by the neck, so violently that she thought her joints were broken. It was a laugh she would never forget, like a vile taunt out of hellish darkness. Mingling with it was another gruesome sound, the awful clanking of armor.

Thomas let go with all his legs at once and tumbled head over heels through the branches into the water-butt.

"I doubt if you get away alive," he called back. But the poor little bee no longer heard.

She couldn't see her assailant, her neck was caught in too firm a grip, but a gilt-sheathed arm passed before her eyes, and a huge head with dreadful pincers suddenly thrust itself above her face. She took it at first to belong to a gigantic wasp, but then realized that she had fallen into the clutches of a hornet. The black-and-yellow striped monster was surely four times her size.

Maya lost sight, hearing, speech; every nerve in her body went faint. At length her voice came back, and she screamed for help.

"Never mind, girlie," said the hornet in a honey-sweet tone that was sickening. "Never mind. It'll last until it's over." He smiled a baleful smile.

"Let go!" cried Maya. "Let me go! Or I'll sting you in your heart."

"In my heart right away? Very brave. But there's time for that later."

Maya went into a fury. Summoning all her strength, she twisted herself around, uttered her shrill battle-cry, and directed her sting against the middle of the hornet's breast. To her amazement and horror, the sting, instead of piercing his breast, swerved on the surface. The brigand's armor was impervious.

Wrath gleamed in his eyes.

"I could bite your head off, little one, to punish you for your impudence. And I would, too, I would indeed, but for our queen. She prefers fresh bees to dead carcasses. So a good soldier saves a juicy morsel like you to bring to her alive."

The hornet, with Maya still in his grip, rose into the air and made directly for the fortress.

"This is too awful," thought the poor little bee. "No one can stand this." She fainted.

When she came to her senses, she found herself in half darkness, in a sultry dusk permeated by a horrid, pungent smell. Slowly everything came back to her. A great paralyzing sadness settled in her heart. She wanted to cry: the tears refused to come.

"I haven't been eaten up yet, but I may be, any moment," she thought in a tremble.

Through the walls of her prison she caught the distinct sound of voices, and soon she noticed that a little light filtered through a narrow chink. The hornets make their walls, not of wax like the bees, but of a dry mass resembling porous grey paper. By the one thread of light she managed bit by bit to make out her surroundings. Horror of horrors! Maya was almost congealed with fright: the floor was strewn with the bodies of dead insects. At her very feet lay a little rose-beetle turned over on its back; to one side was the skeleton of a large locust broken in two, and everywhere were the remains of slaughtered bees, their wings and legs and sheaths.

"Oh, oh, to think this had to happen to me,"
whimpered little Maya. She did not dare to stir the
fraction of an inch and pressed herself shivering
into the farthest corner of this chamber of horrors.

Again she heard voices on the other side of the
wall. Impelled by mortal fear, she crept up to the
chink and peeped through. What she saw was a vast
hall crowded with hornets and magnificently
illuminated by a number of captive glow-worms.
Enthroned in their midst sat the queen, who seemed
to be holding an important council. Maya caught
every word that was said.

If those glittering monsters had not inspired her
with such unspeakable horror, she would have gone
into raptures over their strength and magnificence.
It was the first time she had had a good view of any
of the race of brigands. Tigers they looked like,
superb tigers of the insect world, with their tawny
black-barred bodies. A shiver of awe ran through
the little bee.

A sergeant-at-arms went about the walls of the hall
ordering the glow-worms to give all the light they
could; they must strain themselves to the utmost. He
muttered his commands in a low voice, so as not to
interrupt the deliberations, and thrust at them with a
long spear, hissing as he did so:

"Light up, or I'll eat you!"

Terrible the things that were done in the fortress of
the hornets!

Then Maya heard the queen say:

"Very well, we shall abide by the arrangements we have made. To-morrow, one hour before dawn, the warriors will assemble and sally forth to the attack on the city of the bees in the castle park. The hive is to be plundered and as many prisoners taken as possible. He who captures Queen Helen VIII and brings her to me alive will be dubbed a knight. Go forth and be brave and victorious and bring back rich booty.-- The meeting is herewith adjourned. Sleep well, my warriors. I bid you good-night."

The queen-hornet rose from her throne and left the hall accompanied by her body-guard.

Maya nearly cried out loud.

"My country!" she sobbed, "my bees, my dear, dear bees!" She pressed her hands to her mouth to keep herself from screaming. She was in the depths of despair. "Oh, would that I had died before I heard this. No one will warn my people. They will be attacked in their sleep and massacred. O God, perform a miracle, help me, help me and my people. Our need is great!"

In the hall the glow-worms were put out and devoured. Gradually the fortress was wrapped in a hush. Maya seemed to have been forgotten. A faint twilight crept into her cell, and she thought she caught the strumming of the crickets' night song outside.-- Was anything more horrible than this dungeon with its carcasses strewn on the ground!

CHAPTER XIV

THE SENTINEL

Soon, however, the little bee's despair yielded to a definite resolve. It was as though she once more called to mind that she was a bee.

"Here I am weeping and wailing," she thought, "as if I had no brains and as if I were a weakling. Oh, I'm not much of an honor to my people and my queen. They are in danger. I am doomed anyhow. So since death is certain one way or another, I may as well be proud and brave and do everything I can to try to save them."

It was as though Maya had completely forgotten the long time that had passed since she left her home. More strongly than ever she felt herself one of her people; and the great responsibility that suddenly devolved upon her, through the knowledge of the hornets' plot, filled her with fine courage and determination.

"If my people are to be vanquished and killed, I want to be killed, too. But first I must do everything in my power to save them."

"Long live my queen!" she cried.

"Quiet in there!" clanged harshly from the outside.

Ugh, what an awful voice!-- The watchman making his rounds.-- Then it was already late in the night.

As soon as the watchman's footsteps had died away, Maya began to widen the chink through which she had peeped into the hall. It was easy to bite away the brittle stuff of the partition, though it took some time before the opening was large enough to admit her body. At length, in the full knowledge that discovery would cost her her life, she squeezed through into the hall. From remote depths of the fortress echoed the sound of loud snoring.

The hall lay in a subdued blue light that found its way in through the distant entrance.

"The moonlight!" Maya said to herself. She began to creep cautiously toward the exit, cowering close in the deep shadows of the walls, until she reached the high, narrow passageway that led from the hall to the opening through which the light shone. She heaved a deep sigh. Far, far away glimmered a star.

"Liberty!" she thought.

The passageway was quite bright. Softly, stepping oh so very softly, Maya crept on. The portal came nearer and nearer.

"If I fly now," she thought, "I'll be out in one dash." Her heart pounded as if ready to burst.

But there in the shadow of the doorway stood a sentinel leaning against a column.

Maya stood still, rooted to the spot. Vanished all her hopes. Gone the chance of escape. There was no getting by that formidable figure. What was she to do? Best go back where she had come from. But the sight of the giant in the doorway held her in a spell. He seemed to be lost in revery. He stood gazing out upon the moon-washed landscape, his head tilted slightly forward, his chin propped on his hand. How his golden cuirass gleamed in the moonlight! Something in the way he stood there stirred the little bee's emotions.

"He looks so sad," she thought. "How handsome he is, how superbly he holds himself, how proudly his armor shines! He never removes it, neither by day nor by night. He is always ready to rob and fight and die...."

Little Maya quite forgot that this man was her enemy. Ah, how often the same thing had happened to her--that the goodness of her heart and her delight in beauty made her lose all sense of danger.

A golden dart of light shot from the bandit's helmet. He must have turned his head.

"My God," whispered Maya, "this is the end of me!"

But the sentinel said quietly:

"Just come here, child."

"What!" cried Maya. "You saw me?"

"All the time, child. You bit a hole through the wall, then you crept along--crept along--tucking yourself very neatly into the dark places--until you reached the spot where you're standing. Then you saw me, and you lost heart. Am I right?"

"Yes," said Maya, "quite right." Her whole body shook with terror. The sentinel, then, had seen her the entire time. She remembered having heard how keen were the senses of these clever freebooters.

"What are you doing here?" he asked good-humoredly.

Maya still thought he looked sad. His mind seemed to be far away and not to concern itself with what was of such moment to her.

"I'd like to get out," she answered. "And I'm not afraid. I was just startled. You looked so strong and handsome, and your armor shone so. Now I'll fight you."

The sentinel, slightly astonished, leaned forward, and looked at Maya and smiled. It was not an ugly smile, and Maya experienced an entirely new feeling: the young warrior's smile seemed to exercise a mysterious power over her heart.

"No, little one," he said almost tenderly, "you and I won't fight. You bees belong to a powerful nation, but man for man we hornets are stronger. To do single battle with a bee would be beneath our dignity. If you like you may stay here a little while and chat. But only a little while. Soon I'll have to wake the soldiers up; then, back to your cell you must go."

How curious! The hornet's lofty friendliness
disarmed Maya more than anger or hate could have
done. The feeling with which he inspired her was
almost admiration. With great sad eyes she looked
up at her enemy, and constrained, as always, to
follow the impulses of her heart, she said:

"I have always heard bad things about hornets. But
you are not bad. I can't believe you're bad."

The warrior looked at Maya.

"There are good people and bad people
everywhere," he said, gravely. "But you mustn't
forget we are your enemies, and shall always
remain your enemies."

"Must an enemy always be bad?" asked Maya.
"Before, when you were looking out into the
moonlight, I forgot that you were hard and
dangerous. You seemed sad, and I have always
thought that people who were sad couldn't possibly
be wicked."

The sentinel said nothing, and Maya continued
more boldly:

"You are powerful. If you want to, you can put me
back in my cell, and I'll have to die. But you can
also set me free--if you want to."

At this the warrior drew himself up. His armor
clanked, and the arm he raised shone in the
moonlight.

But the moonlight was turning dimmer in the passageway. Was dawn coming already?

"You are right," he said. "I can. My people and my queen have entrusted me with this power. My orders are that no bee who has set foot in this fortress shall leave it alive. I shall keep faith with my people."

After a pause he added softly as if to himself: "I have learned by bitter experience how faithlessness can hurt--when Loveydear forsook me...."

Little Maya was overcome. She did not know what to say. Ah, the same sentiments moved her, too-- love of her own kind, loyalty to her people. Nothing to be done here but to use force or strategy. Each did his duty, and yet each remained an enemy to the other.

But hadn't the sentinel mentioned a name? Hadn't he said something about someone's having been unfaithful to him? Loveydear--why, she knew Loveydear--the beautiful dragon-fly who lived at the lakeside among the waterlilies.

Maya quivered with excitement. Here, perhaps, was her salvation. But she wasn't quite sure how much good her knowledge would be to her. So she said prudently:

"Who is Loveydear, if I may ask?"

"Never mind, little one. She's not your affair, and she's lost to me forever. I shall never find her again."

"I know Miss Loveydear." Maya forced herself to put the utmost indifference into her tone. "She belongs to the family of dragon-flies and she's the loveliest lady of all."

A tremendous change came over the warrior. He seemed to have forgotten where he was. He leapt over to Maya's sides as if blown by a violent gust.

"What! You know Loveydear? Tell me where she is. Tell me, right away."

"No."

Maya spoke quietly and firmly; she glowed with secret delight.

"I'll bite your head off if you don't tell." The warrior drew dangerously close.

"It will be bitten off anyhow. Go ahead. I shan't betray the lovely dragon-fly. She's a close friend of mine.... You want to imprison her."

The warrior breathed hard. In the gathering dawn Maya could see that his forehead was pale and his eyes tragic with the inner struggle he was waging.

"Good God!" he said wildly. "It's time to rouse the soldiers.-- No, no, little bee, I don't want to harm Loveydear. I love her, more dearly than my life. Tell me where I shall find her again."

Maya was clever. She purposely hesitated before she said:

"But I love my life."

"If you tell me where Loveydear lives"--Maya could see that the sentinel spoke with difficulty and was trembling all over-- "I'll set you free. You can fly wherever you want."

"Will you keep your word?"

"My word of honor as a brigand," said the sentinel proudly.

Maya could scarcely speak. But, if she was to be in time to warn her people of the attack, every moment counted. Her heart exulted.

"Very well," she said, "I believe you. Listen, then. Do you know the ancient linden-trees near the castle? Beyond them lies one meadow after another, and finally comes a big lake. In a cove at the south end where the brook empties into the lake the waterlilies lie spread out on the water in the sunlight. Near them, in the rushes, is where Loveydear lives. You'll find her there every day at noon when the sun is high in the heavens."

The warrior had pressed both hands to his pale brow. He seemed to be having a desperate struggle with himself.

"You're telling the truth," he said softly and

groaned, whether from joy or pain it was impossible to tell. "She told me she wanted to go where there were floating white flowers. Those must be the flowers you speak of. Fly away, then. I thank you."

And actually he stepped aside from the entrance.

Day was breaking.

"A brigand keeps his word," he said.

Not knowing that Maya had overheard the deliberations in the council chamber, he told himself that one small bee more or less made little difference. Weren't there hundreds of others?

"Good-by," cried Maya, breathless with haste, and flew off without a word of thanks.

As a matter of fact, there was no time to spare.

CHAPTER XV

THE WARNING

Little Maya summoned every bit of strength and will power she had left. Like a bullet shot from the muzzle of a gun (bees can fly faster than most insects), she darted through the purpling dawn in a lightning beeline for the woods, where she knew she would be safe for the moment and could hide herself away should the hornet regret having let her go and follow in pursuit.

Gossamer veils hung everywhere over the level country, big drops fell from the trees on the dry leaves carpeting the ground, and the cold in the woods threatened to paralyze little Maya's wings. No ray of the dawn had as yet found its way between the trees. The air was as hushed as if the sun had forgotten the earth, and all creatures had laid themselves to eternal rest.

Maya, therefore, flew high up in the air. Only one thing mattered--to get back as quickly as strength and wits permitted to her hive, her people, her endangered home. She must warn her people. They must prepare against the attack which the terrible brigands had planned for that very morning. Oh, if only the nation of bees had the chance to arm and make ready its defenses, it was well able to cope with its stronger opponents. But a surprise assault at rising time! What if the queen and the soldiers were still asleep? The success of the hornets would then be assured. They would take prisoners and give no quarter. The butchery would be horrible.

Thinking of the strength and energy of her people, their readiness to meet death, their devotion to their queen, the little bee felt a great wrath against their enemies the hornets. Her beloved people! No sacrifice was too great for them. Little Maya's heart swelled with the ecstasy of self-sacrifice and the dauntless courage of enthusiasm.

It was not easy for her to find her way over the woods. Long before she had ceased to observe landmarks as did the other bees, who had great distances to come back with their loads of nectar.

She felt she had never flown as high before, the cold hurt, and she could scarcely distinguish the objects below.

"What can I go by?" she thought. "No one thing stands out. I shan't be able to reach my people and help them. Oh, oh! And here I had a chance to atone for my desertion. What shall I do? What shall I do?"-- Suddenly some secret force steered her in a certain direction. "*What* is pushing and pulling me? It must be homesickness guiding me back to my country." She gave herself up to the instinct and flew swiftly on. Soon, in the distance, looking like grey domes in the dim light of the dawn, showed the mighty lindens of the castle park. She exclaimed with delight. She knew where she was. She dropped closer to the earth. In the meadows on one side hung the luminous wisps of fog, thicker here than in the woods. She thought of the flower-sprites who cheerfully died their early death inside the floating veils. That inspired her anew with confidence. Her anxiety disappeared. Let her people spurn her from the kingdom, let the queen punish her for desertion, if only the bees were spared this dreadful calamity of the hornets' invasion.

Close to the long stone wall shone the silver-fir that shielded the bee-city against the west wind. And there--she could see them distinctly now--were the red, blue, and green portals of her homeland. The stormy pounding of her heart nearly robbed her of her breath. But on she flew toward the red entrance which led to her people and her queen.

On the flying-board, two sentinels blocked the

entrance and laid hands upon her. Maya was too breathless to utter a syllable, and the sentinels threatened to kill her. For a bee to force its way into a strange city without the queen's consent is a capital offense.

"Stand back!" cried one sentinel, thrusting her roughly away. "What's the matter with you! If you don't leave this instant, you'll die.-- Did you ever!" He turned to the other sentinel. "Have you ever seen the like, and before daytime too?"

Now Maya pronounced the password by which all the bees knew one another. The sentinels instantly released her.

"What!" they cried. "You are one of us, and we don't know you?"

"Let me get to the queen," groaned the little bee. "Right away, quick! We are in terrible danger."

The sentinels still hesitated. They couldn't grasp the situation.

"The queen may not be awakened before sunrise," said the one.

"Then," Maya screamed, her voice rising to a passionate yell such as the sentinels had probably never heard from a bee before, "then the queen will never wake up alive. Death is following at my heels. Take me to the queen! Take me to the queen, I say!" Her voice was so wild and wrathful that the sentinels were frightened, and obeyed.

The three hurried together through the warm, well-
known streets and corridors. Maya recognized
everything, and for all her excitement and the
tremendous need for haste, her heart quivered with
sweet melancholy at the sight of the dear familiar
scenes.

"I am at home," she stammered with pale lips.

In the queen's reception room she almost broke
down. One of the sentinels supported her while the
other hurried with the unusual message into the
private chambers. Both of them now realized that
something momentous was taking place, and the
messenger ran as fast as his legs would carry him.

The first wax-generators were already up. Here and
there a little head thrust itself out curiously from the
openings. The news of the incident traveled quickly.

Two officers emerged from the private chambers.
Maya recognized them instantly. In solemn silence,
without a word to her, they took their posts, one on
each side of the doorway: the queen would soon
appear.

She came without her court, attended only by her
aide and two ladies-in-waiting. She hurried straight
over to Maya. When she saw what a state the child
was in, the severe expression on her face relaxed a
little.

"You have come with an important message? Who
are you?"

Maya could not speak at once. Finally she managed to frame two words:

"The hornets!"

The queen turned pale. But her composure was unshaken, and Maya was somewhat calmed.

"Almighty queen!" she cried. "Forgive me for not respecting the duties I owe Your Majesty. Later I will tell you everything I have done. I repent. With my whole heart I repent.-- Just a little while ago, as by a miracle, I escaped from the fortress of the hornets, and the last I heard was that they were planning to attack and plunder our kingdom at dawn."

The wild dismay that the little bee's words produced was indescribable. The ladies-in-waiting set up a loud wail, the officers at the door turned pale and made as if to dash off and sound the alarm, the aide said: "Good God!" and wheeled completely round, because he wanted to see on all sides at once.

As for the queen, it was really extraordinary to see with what composure, what resourcefulness she received the dreadful news. She drew herself up, and there was something in her attitude that both intimidated and inspired endless confidence. Little Maya was awed. Never, she felt, had she witnessed anything so superior. It was like a great, magnificent event in itself.

The queen beckoned the officers to her side and uttered a few rapid sentences aloud. At the end

Maya heard:

"I give you one minute for the execution of my
orders. A fraction of a second longer, and it will
cost you your heads."

But the officers scarcely looked as if they needed
this incentive. In less time than it takes to tell they
were gone. Their instant readiness was a joy to
behold.

"O my queen!" said Maya.

The queen inclined her head to the little bee, who
once again for a brief moment saw her monarch's
countenance beam upon her gently, lovingly.

"You have our thanks," she said. "You have saved
us. No matter what your previous conduct may have
been, you have made up for it a thousandfold.-- But
go, rest now, little girl, you look very miserable,
and your hands are trembling."

"I should like to die for you," Maya stammered,
quivering.

"Don't worry about us," replied the queen. "Among
the thousands inhabiting this city there is not one
who would hesitate a moment to sacrifice his life
for me and for the welfare of the country. You can
go to sleep peacefully."

She bent over and kissed the little bee on her
forehead. Then she beckoned to the ladies-in-

waiting and bade them see to Maya's rest and comfort.

Maya, stirred to the depths of her being, allowed herself to be led away. After this, life had nothing lovelier to offer. As in a dream she heard the loud, clear signals in the distance, saw the high dignitaries of state assemble around the royal chambers, heard a dull, far-echoing drone that shook the hive from roof to foundation.

"The soldiers! Our soldiers!" whispered the ladies-in-waiting at her side.

The last thing Maya heard in the little room where her companions put her to bed was the tramp of soldiers marching past her door and commands shouted in a blithe, resolute, ringing voice. Into her dreams, echoing as from a great distance, she carried the ancient song of the soldier-bees:

Sunlight, sunlight, golden sheen, By your glow our lives are lighted; Bless our labors, bless our Queen, Let us always be united.

CHAPTER XVI

THE BATTLE

The kingdom of the bees was in a whirl of excitement. Not even in the days of the revolution had the turmoil been so great. The hive rumbled and roared. Every bee was fired by a holy wrath, a burning ardor to meet and fight the ancient enemy to the very last gasp. Yet there was no disorder or confusion. Marvelous the speed with which the regiments were mobilized, marvelous the way each soldier knew his duty and fell into his right place and took up his right work.

It was high time. At the queen's call for volunteers to defend the entrance, a number of bees offered themselves, and of these several had been sent out to see if the enemy was approaching. Two had now returned--whizzing dots--and reported that the hornets were drawing near.

An awesome hush of expectancy fell upon the hive. Soldiers in three closed ranks stood lined up at the entrance, proud, pale, solemn, composed. No one spoke. The silence of death prevailed, except for the low commands of the officers drawing up the reserves in the rear. The hive seemed to be fast asleep. The only stir came from the doorway where about a dozen wax-generators were at work in feverish silence executing their orders to narrow the entrance with wax. As by a miracle, two thick partitions of wax had already gone up, which even the strongest hornets could not batter down without great loss of time. The hole had been reduced by almost half.

The queen took up an elevated position inside the hive from which she was able to survey the battle. Her aides flew scurrying hither and thither.

The third messenger returned. He sank down exhausted at the queen's feet.

"I am the last who will return," he shouted with all the strength he had left. "The others have been killed."

"Where are the hornets?" asked the queen.

"At the lindens!-- Listen, listen," he stammered in mortal terror, "the air hums with the wings of the giants."

No sound was heard. It must have been the poor fellow's terrified imagination, he must have thought he was still being pursued.

"How many are there?" asked the queen sternly. "Answer in a low voice."

"I counted forty."

Although the queen was startled by the enemy's numbers, she gave no sign of shock.

In a ringing, confident voice that all could hear, she said:

"Not one of them will see his home again."

Her words, which seemed to sound the enemy's doom, had instant effect. Men and officers alike felt their courage rise.

But when in the quiet of the morning an ominous whirring was heard outside the hive, first softly, then louder and louder, and the entrance darkened, and the whispering voices of the hornets, the most frightful robbers and murderers in the insect world, penetrated into the hive, then the faces of the valiant little bees turned pale as if washed over by a drab light falling upon their ranks. They gazed at one another with eyes in which death sat waiting, and those who were ranged at the entrance knew full well that one moment more and all would be over with them.

The queen's controlled voice came clear and tranquil from her place on high:

"Let the robbers enter one by one until I give orders to attack. Then those at the front throw themselves upon the invaders a hundred at a time, and the ranks behind cover the entrance. In that way we shall divide up the enemy's forces. Remember, you at the front, upon your strength and endurance and bravery depends the fate of the whole state. Have no fear; in the dusk the enemy will not see right away how well prepared we are, and he will enter unsuspecting...."

She broke off. There, thrust through the doorway, was the head of the first brigand. The feelers played about, groping, cautious, the pincers opened and closed. It was a blood-curdling sight. Slowly the huge black-and-gold striped body with its strong wings crept in after the head. The light falling in from the outside drew gleams from the warrior's cuirass.

Something like a quiver went through the ranks of the bees, but the silence remained unbroken.

The hornet withdrew quietly. Outside he could be heard announcing:

"They're fast asleep. But the entrance is half walled up and there are no sentinels. I do not know whether to take this as a good or a bad sign."

"A good sign!" rang out. "Forward!"

At that two giants leapt in through the entrance side by side; after them, soundlessly, pressed a throng of striped, armed, gleaming warriors, awful to behold. Eight made their way into the hive. Still no orders to attack from the queen. Was she dumb with horror, had her voice failed her?

And the brigands, did they not see in the shadow, to right and left, the soldiers drawn up in close, glittering ranks ready for mortal combat...?

Now at last came the order from on high:

"In the name of eternal right, in the name of your queen, to the defense of the realm!"

At that a droning roar went up. Never before had the city been shaken by such a battle-cry. It threatened to burst the hive in two. Where, an instant before, the hornets had been visible singly, there were now buzzing heaps, thick, dark, rolling knots. A young officer had scarcely awaited the end of the queen's words. He wanted to be the first to attack. He was the first to die. He had stood for some time ready to leap all a-quiver with eagerness for battle, and at the first sound of the order he rushed forward right into the clutches of the foremost brigand. His delicately fine-pointed sting found its way between the head and upper breast-ring of his opponent; he heard the hornet give a yell of rage, saw him double up into a glittering, gold-black ball. Then the bandit's fearful sting leapt out and pierced between the young officer's breast-rings right into his heart; and dying the bee felt himself and his mortally wounded enemy sink under a cloud of storming bees. His brave death inspired them all with the wild rapture that comes from utter willingness to die for a noble cause. Fearful was their attack upon the invaders. The hornets were sore pressed.

But the hornets are an old race of robbers, trained to warfare. Pillage and murder have long been their gruesome profession. Though the initial assault of the bees had confused and divided them, yet the damage was not so great as might have seemed at first. For the bees' stings did not penetrate their breastplates, and their strength and gigantic size gave them an advantage of which they were well aware. Their sharp, buzzing battle-cry rose high above the battle-cry of the bees. It is a sound that fills all creatures with horror, even human beings, who dread this danger signal, and are careful not to enter into conflict with hornets unprotected.

Those of the assailants who had already penetrated into the hive quickly realized that they must make their way still deeper inward if they were not to block up the entrance to their comrades outside. And so the struggling knots rolled farther and farther down the dark streets and corridors. How right the queen had been in her tactics! No sooner was a bit of space at the entrance cleared than the ranks in the rear leapt forward to its defense. It was an old strategy, and a dreadful one for the enemy. When a hornet at the entrance gave signs of exhaustion, the bees shammed the same, and let him crawl in; but the instant the one behind showed his head a great swarm of fresh soldiers dashed up to defend the apparently unprotected entrance, while the invader who had gone on ahead would find himself, already wearied, suddenly confronted by glittering ranks of soldier-bees who had not yet stirred a finger in battle. Generally he succumbed to their superior numbers at the very first attack.

Now the groans of the wounded and the shrieks of the dying mingled in wild agony with the fierce battle-cries. The hornets' stings worked fearful havoc among the bees. The rolling knots left tracks of dead bodies in their wake. The hornets, whose retreat had been cut off, realizing that they would never see the light of day again, fought the fight of despair. Yet, slowly, one by one, they succumbed. There was one great thing against them. Though their strength was inexhaustible, not so the poison of their sting. After a time their sting lost its virulence, and the wounded bees, knowing they'd recover, fought in the consciousness of certain victory. To this was added the grief of the bees for their dead; it gave them the power of divine wrath.

Gradually the din subsided. The loud calls of the hornets on the outside met with no response from the invaders within.

"They are all dead," said the leader of the hornets grimly, and summoned the combatants back from the entrance. Their numbers had melted down to half.

"We have been betrayed," said the leader. "The bees were prepared."

The hornets were assembled on the silver-fir. It had grown lighter, and the red of dawn tinged the tops of the linden-trees. The birds began to sing. The dew fell. Pale and quivering with rage of battle, the warriors stood around their leader, who was waging an awful inward struggle. Should he yield to prudence or to his lust for pillage? The former prevailed. There was no use anyway. His whole tribe was in danger of destruction. Grudgingly, in a shudder of thwarted ambition, he determined to send a messenger to the bees to sue for the return of the prisoners.

He chose his cleverest officer and called upon him by name.

A depressed silence instead of an answer. The officer was among those who had been cut off.

The leader, overcome now by mortal dread lest those who had entered would never return, quickly chose another officer. The raging and roaring in the beehive could be heard in the distance.

"Be quick!" he cried, laying the white petal of a jasmine in the messenger's hand, "or the human beings will soon come and we shall be lost. Tell the bees we will go away and leave them in peace forever if they will deliver up the prisoners."

The messenger rushed off. At the entrance he waved his white signal and alighted on the flying-board.

The queen-bee was immediately informed that an emissary was outside who wanted to make terms, and she sent her aide to parley with him. When he returned with his report she sent back this reply:

"We will deliver up the dead if you want to take them away. There are no prisoners. All of your people who invaded our territory are dead. Your promise never to return we do not believe. You may come again, whenever you wish. You will fare no better than you did to-day. And if you want to go on with the battle we are ready to fight to the last bee."

The leader of the hornets turned pale when this message was delivered to him. He clenched his fists, he fought with himself. Only too gladly would he have yielded to the wishes of his warriors who clamored for revenge. Reason prevailed.

"We *will* come again," he hissed. "How could this thing have happened to us? Are we not a more powerful people than the bees? Every campaign of mine so far has been successful and has only added to our glory. How can I face the queen after this defeat?" In a quiver of fury he cried again: "How could this thing have happened to us? There must be treachery somewhere."

An older hornet known as a friend of the queen's here took up the word.

"It is true, we *are* a more powerful race, but the bees are a unified nation, and unflinchingly loyal to their people and their state. That is a great source of strength; it makes them irresistible. Not one of them would turn traitor; each without thought of self serves the weal of all."

The leader scarcely listened.

"My day is coming," he hissed. "What care I for the wisdom of these bourgeois! I am a brigand and will die a brigand.-- But to keep up the battle now would be madness. What good would it do us if we destroyed the whole hive, and none of us came back alive?" Turning to the messenger, he cried:

"Give us back our dead. We will withdraw."

A dead silence fell. The messenger flew off.

"We must be prepared for a fresh piece of trickery, though I don't think the hornets are in a fighting mood at present," said the queen bee when she heard the hornets' decision. She gave orders for the rear-guard, wax-generators, and honey-carriers to remove the dead from the city while two fresh regiments guarded the entrance.

Her orders were carried out. Over mountains of the dead one brigand's body after another was dragged to the entrance and thrown to the ground outside.

In gloomy silence the troop of hornets waited on the silver-fir and saw the corpses of their fallen warriors drop one by one to the earth.

The sun arose upon a scene of endless desolation. Twenty-one slain, who had died a glorious death, made a heap in the grass under the city of the bees. Not a drop of honey, not a single prisoner had been taken by the enemy. The hornets picked up their dead and flew away, the battle was over, the bees had conquered.

But at what a cost! Everywhere lay fallen bodies, in the streets and corridors, in the dim places before the brooders and honey-cupboards. Sad was the work in the hive on that lovely morning of summer sunshine and scented blossoms. The dead had to be disposed of, the wounded had to be bandaged and nursed. But before the hour of noon had struck, the regular tasks were begun; for the bees neither celebrated their victory nor spent time mourning their dead. Each bee carried his pride and his grief locked quietly in his breast and went about his work.

CHAPTER XVII

THE QUEEN'S FRIEND

The noise of battle awoke Maya out of a brief sleep. She jumped up and straightway wanted to dash out to help defend the city, but soon realized that she was too weak to be of any help.

A group of struggling combatants came rolling
toward her. One of them was a strong young hornet,
an officer, Maya judged by his badge, who was
defending himself unaided against an overwhelming
number of bees. The struggling knot drew nearer.
To Maya's horror it left one dead bee after another
in its wake. But numbers finally told against the
giant: whole clusters of bees, ready to die rather
than let go, hung to his arms and legs and feelers,
and their stings were beginning to pierce between
the rings of his breast. Maya saw him drop down
exhausted. Without cry or complaint, fighting to the
very end, neither suing for mercy nor reviling his
opponents, he went down to his brigand's death.

The bees left him and hurried back to the entrance
to throw themselves anew into the conflict.

Maya's heart was beating stormily. She slipped over
to the hornet. He lay curled up in the twilight, still
breathing. She counted about twenty stings, most of
them in the fore part of his body, leaving his golden
armor quite whole and sound. Seeing he was still
alive, she hurried away to bring water and honey--to
cheer the dying man, she thought. But he shook his
head and waived her off with his hand.

"I *take* what I want," he said proudly. "I don't care
for gifts."

"Oh," said Maya, "I only thought you might be
thirsty."

The young officer smiled at her, then said, not
sadly, but with a strange earnestness:

"I must die."

The little bee could not reply. For the first time in
her life she seemed to comprehend what it meant to
have to die; and death seemed much closer when
someone else was about to die than when her own
life had been imperiled in the spider's web.

"If there were only *some*thing I could do," she said,
and burst into tears.

The dying hornet made no answer. He opened his
eyes once again and heaved a deep breath--for the
last time. Half an hour later he was thrown down
into the grass outside the hive along with his dead
comrades.

Little Maya never forgot what she had learned from
this brief farewell. She knew now for all time that
her enemies were beings like herself, loving life as
she did and having to die a hard death without
succor. She thought of the flower sprite who had
told her of his rebirth when Nature sent forth her
blossoms again in the spring; and she longed to
know whether the other creatures would, like the
sprite, come back to the light of life after they had
died the death of the earth.

"I will believe it is so," she said softly.

A messenger now came and summoned her to the
queen's presence. She found the full court

assembled in the royal reception room. Her legs shook, she scarcely dared to raise her eyes before her monarch and so many dignitaries. A number of the officers of the queen's staff were missing, and the gathering was unusually solemn. Yet a gleam of exaltation seemed to light every brow--as if the consciousness of triumph and new glory won encircled everyone like an invisible halo.

The queen arose, made her way unattended through the assemblage, went up to little Maya and took her in her arms.

This Maya had never expected, not this. The measure of her joy was full to overflowing; she broke down and wept.

The bees were deeply stirred. There was not one among them who did not share Maya's happiness, who was not deeply grateful for the little bee's valiant deed.

Maya now had to tell her whole story. Everybody wanted to know how she had learned of the hornets' plans and how she had succeeded in breaking out of the awful prison from which no bee had ever before escaped.

So Maya told of all the remarkable things she had seen and heard, of Miss Loveydear with the glittering wings, of the grasshopper, of Thekla the spider, of Puck, and of how splendidly Bobbie had come to her rescue. When she told of the sprite and the human beings, it was so quiet in the hall that you could hear the generators in the back of the hive kneading the wax.

"Ah," said the queen, "who'd have thought the sprites were so lovely?" She smiled to herself with a look of melancholy and longing, as people will who long for beauty.

And all the dignitaries smiled the same smile.

"How did the song of the sprite go?" she asked. "Say it again. I'd like to learn it by heart."

Maya repeated the song of the sprite.

My soul is that which breathes anew From all of loveliness and grace; And as it flows from God's own face, It flows from his creations, too.

There was silence for a while. The only sound was a restrained sobbing in the back of the hall--probably someone thinking of a friend who had been killed.

Maya went on with her story. When she came to the hornets, the bees' eyes darkened and widened. Each imagined himself in the situation in which one of their number had been, and quivered, and drew a deep breath.

"Awful," said the queen, "perfectly awful...."

The dignitaries murmured something to the same effect.

"And so," Maya ended, "I reached home. And I sue

for your Majesty's pardon--a thousand times."

Oh, no one bore the little bee any ill will for having run away from the hive. You may imagine they did not.

The queen put her arm round Maya's neck.

"You did not forget your home and your people," she said kindly. "In your heart you were loyal. So we will be loyal to you. Henceforth you shall stay by my side and help me conduct the affairs of state. In that way, I think, your experiences, all the things you have learned, will be made to serve the greatest good of your people and your country."

Cheers of approval greeted the queen's words.

So ends the story of the adventures of Maya the bee. They say her work contributed greatly to the good and welfare of the nation, and she came to be highly respected and loved by her people. Sometimes on quiet evenings she went for a brief hour's conversation to Cassandra's peaceful little room, where the ancient dame lived now on pension honey. There Maya told the young bees, who listened to her eagerly, stories of the adventures which we have lived through with her.

Made in the USA
San Bernardino, CA
12 December 2015